A secret discovery

I moved the flashlight around the tiny room. In one corner of the space, a candle in a tin candleholder sat in a pool of dusty, hardened wax. Just over the candle hung an old black-and-white photograph. It was a picture of a family—a mom, dad, three girls and a baby. A necklace was draped from the same nail that held the photo. It was a simple silver chain so old that it was muddy-black. A pearl circled with little diamonds dangled from the chain. I touched the pearl and set it swinging back and forth like the pendulum on a clock. I guessed it was the first time it had moved in decades.

On the wall opposite the candle, a beat-up book lay tucked between two wall beams. I picked it up. It had a butterfly-wing-blue cover with the word *Journal* printed in gold letters. Someone had scribbled a note on the inside cover of the book. It said,

> *To whoever finds this journal,*
>
> *I'm leaving this book behind on purpose. All the bad things in the world lie inked on these pages, and at the present, I don't want to remember.*
>
> *Sincerely,*
> *Helen White*

OTHER BOOKS YOU MAY ENJOY

Palace Beautiful

Sarah DeFord Williams

PUFFIN BOOKS
An Imprint of Penguin Group (USA) Inc.

For Simon, Ellen and Charlotte

PUFFIN BOOKS
Published by the Penguin Group
Penguin Young Readers Group, 345 Hudson Street, New York, New York 10014, U.S.A.
Penguin Group (Canada), 90 Eglinton Avenue East, Suite 700, Toronto, Ontario, Canada M4P 2Y3
(a division of Pearson Penguin Canada Inc.)
Penguin Books Ltd, 80 Strand, London WC2R 0RL, England
Penguin Ireland, 25 St Stephen's Green, Dublin 2, Ireland (a division of Penguin Books Ltd)
Penguin Group (Australia), 250 Camberwell Road, Camberwell, Victoria 3124, Australia
(a division of Pearson Australia Group Pty Ltd)
Penguin Books India Pvt Ltd, 11 Community Centre, Panchsheel Park, New Delhi - 110 017, India
Penguin Group (NZ), 67 Apollo Drive, Rosedale, North Shore 0632, New Zealand
(a division of Pearson New Zealand Ltd)
Penguin Books (South Africa) (Pty) Ltd, 24 Sturdee Avenue,
Rosebank, Johannesburg 2196, South Africa

Registered Offices: Penguin Books Ltd, 80 Strand, London WC2R 0RL, England

First published in the United States of America by G. P. Putnam's Sons,
a division of Penguin Young Readers Group, 2010
Published by Puffin Books, a division of Penguin Young Readers Group, 2011

3 5 7 9 10 8 6 4 2

THE LIBRARY OF CONGRESS HAS CATALOGED THE PUTNAM EDITION AS FOLLOWS:
Williams, Sarah DeFord.
Palace beautiful / Sarah DeFord Williams.
p. cm.
Summary: After their move in 1985 to Salt Lake City, thirteen-year-old Sadie finds a journal in a hidey-hole in
the attic, and with her sister and new friend they read about the influenza epidemic of 1918.
ISBN: 978-0-399-25298-3 (hc)
[1. Moving, Household—Fiction. 2. Diaries—Fiction. 3. Influenza Epidemic, 1918–1919—Fiction.
4. Family life—Utah—Fiction. 5. Salt Lake City (Utah)—History—20th century—Fiction.]
I. Title
PZ7.W6681737Pal 2010
[Fic]—dc22 2009003213

Puffin Books ISBN 978-0-14-241745-4

Text set in Cg Cloister
Printed in the United States of America

M**Y NAME IS SADIE EVELYN BROOKS.** I'm thirteen years old and practically a woman. I love painting, Frosty Cocoa Flakes cereal and my family. I hate stomachaches, spiders and saying good-bye. July 5, 1985." That's what I wrote on the inside of my bathroom cabinet just before we hopped in the car to leave Texas for good. That way, even if it was just in the bathroom, I'd always be a part of the story of the house where I used to live.

Far-Far-Away Blue

MY SISTER ZUZU SAYS NO ONE CAN remember the day they were born, but I do. The day I was born, my mother told me the story of how people came into being. As she spoke, the story felt warm and soft like her skin, her voice and her smile, so I knew it was true. The story went like this:

In the beginning, there was nothing, no light, no dark, no air—nothing. Then, suddenly, a Great Dog as big as the universe came into being and then there was something. His hairs were black, and each one was as big as a hundred planets. His teeth were white and filled his immense red mouth, which was as large as a thousand galaxies.

The dog panted and howled with loneliness. He lay his head down on one paw and fell asleep, and as he slept, his dreams leaked from his ear and spilled out over the nothingness. Out came planets, stars, moons, solar systems, water, day and night, trees, monkeys, crab apples, lightning bugs and people. The entire universe spilled out of his dreams. When he woke, he howled with joy. Then there was everything.

I remember the way my mother's breath tickled my ear as she whispered the story. Her long brown hair hung damp and messy down her shoulders. Now and then a strand fell over my face and stuck to my brand-new cheeks. She smelled like roses. I still love the feel of velvety rose petals against my cheeks. It helps me remember.

When a girl loses her mother, nothing is ever the same. Ever. She needs new things, soft things, to fill the empty gaps, and she needs to work as hard as she can to remember.

"I get to choose my room first!" Zuzu shouted as we parked in the street in front of our new home. Dad turned off the car, and the rumbling of the engine and the song "We Are the World," which we had heard at least ten times on our drive, cut off. It felt unnaturally still and quiet.

"Now, Zuzu, we agreed you and Sadie would draw straws," Dad said, craning his neck to look at us in the backseat. He rubbed the back of his neck with his thick palm and tilted his head until his neck popped and cracked like old wood. Sherrie slept restlessly beside him.

Dad found Sherrie a year and a half ago. She came from Nieman Marcus in Dallas. Dad saw her working at the makeup counter and they fell in love. He brought her home one day all dressed up with a big red bow on her head like she was a store-bought present. Sherrie's nice. She smiles a lot and she smells pretty—like expensive shoes. They got married, and now Sherrie's seven and a half months pregnant.

"It's no fair, Daddy! Sadie always wins straws!" shouted Zuzu, kicking the front seat with her Sunday shoes that she wore every day of the week. "She gets to do everything she wants and I never get to do anything but chores!"

"You never do chores," I said, leaning back in my seat. This was going to take a while.

"Yes, I do, Sadie! I wish I was in Jennifer Meyer's family," Zuzu continued. "They let her do anything she wants! She isn't a maid! She isn't second all the time! She isn't treated like a baby! Life is so unfair!"

"Maybe if you didn't act like a baby, we wouldn't treat you like one," I said.

"FINE!" shouted Zuzu. She crossed her arms hard and slammed against the back of her seat.

My mother and I both came from the Great Dog. My sister Zuzu has a different story. My mother died giving birth to her, so the nurses had to whisper her first story, and nurses are poor substitutes for mothers.

Each person has their own first story that they hear right after they take their first gulp of air.

There's the one about Adam and Eve. In the beginning there was nothing. Then God decided to make the universe, so he did, and he liked it. Then He made two people: Adam and Eve. They lived in a beautiful garden, but didn't appreciate it because they didn't know better. Then one day, they ate some fruit that they weren't even supposed to touch, but they did anyway and they started to understand things. The first thing they understood was that they were naked. They felt so embarrassed, they had to run and hide. After a while, though, they started to see and to hear and to taste and to touch and to smell and to understand. They became wise.

There's a story about red birds, but it starts with an apple tree. The tree lived in an orchard. It was very happy. It held its arms wide and each dripped with apples as round as the earth and as red as a ruby. One day a storm tore through the branches of the apple tree. When the wind hushed and the rain stopped, seventy-seven of the tree's apples lay in the dirt, torn too early from the limbs that loved them. The tree wept and its arms felt empty. Just then, seventy-seven beautiful birds as round as the earth and as red as rubies came from the clouds and landed on the branches. Their feathers brushed off the raindrops, and the tree felt happy to have full arms again.

Then there're the people that come from the cabbage patch. Cabbages sit on the ground where they sprouted and never move until someone makes them. Their roots are deep, firm and solid, and their heads are hard. They don't do much looking past their very own patch of dirt, and they don't appreciate being taken from it. People from the cabbage patch can be stubborn and hardheaded like a cabbage. That's where Zuzu came from. That's why she spends so much time with her feet firmly rooted to the floor, crossing her arms and shouting "FINE!" like there's no other way to think about things.

Dad didn't come from anywhere. He was just there waiting like the tree for the red birds when my mom and then Sherrie went looking for a husband. I suppose some people come from somewhere and other people are just waiting for them with their arms wide. Dad is one of the waiting ones.

Another story is one I heard a few years ago in health class. I don't want to write it here because it might shock you. We had to bring permission slips signed by our parents just to hear that story, and when I did hear it, I was so embarrassed, I felt just like Adam and Eve.

A person can always tell what story another person heard first by the way they live. People who hear the Great Dog story first are sometimes lonely. They howl in their own ways for what they miss and need to express themselves any way they can. Sometimes they end up as artists like me.

A person who first hears the Adam and Eve story always looks at their feet and blushes like they are embarrassed. Sometimes they pretend they are something they aren't so people won't know how embarrassed they are. Others open their eyes and ears and become wise and happy. Those who are from the red birds keep trying to fill in the empty spaces left by the loss of something they loved.

Each story comes to a person for a reason and it helps that person find their place. The stories are meant to be remembered. My mom said if a person thinks really hard way back to the day they were born—thinking not only with their head, but their eyes, ears, nose, mouth and fingers—they will remember and their great question will be answered. The key to it all is to remember.

• • •

I stared out the window at the new house. *New* is an entirely relative term. Our house in Houston was built in 1971, the year before I was born, and we had lived in it all my life.

But the houses in Salt Lake City looked very different from the houses in Houston. This house looked like it was a million years old. It's pretty, don't get me wrong. It's red brick with white wood trim like the gingerbread and frosting of a fairy tale house, but it is definitely not "new." Grandma Brooks has lived in the neighborhood for decades and decades. She probably rode past this house in a horse and buggy. Grandma Brooks was the reason we moved to Salt Lake City. She's old. Her health is still good, but she sometimes feels uneasy about living in her very own state away from us. Grandpa Brooks died ten years ago and she has been living alone ever since. She's the kind of lady who makes the most of stuff no matter if it's good or bad.

Our house sat on top of a little hill all its own. A small brick path lined with round bushes stretched from the sidewalk at the bottom of the little hill all the way to the front porch. It almost looked like the house was reaching for us and was glad to see us, like it needed new people to fill it up. I knew right away that I loved it. I knew right away that this was my home.

I looked up at all the windows and wondered who had looked out those windows before. I wondered if a long time ago, another girl saw this house for the first time and knew it was home. I wondered if a home can belong to so many people that even when they move away, the house still misses them.

"We said we'd draw straws, and that's what we'll do," said Dad.

Zuzu crossed her arms fiercely and pouted.

Dad kissed Sherrie on the forehead. "We're here," he said.

Sherrie woke up blinking and yawning. She sighed, rubbed her round belly, leaned over and kissed Dad right back.

Dad took two stubby pencils from the glove box. He stuffed them in his fist.

"Whoever gets the smallest pencil gets to choose a room first."

I drew the bigger one. Zuzu dashed out of the car and scrambled up the front walk. She stood on the front steps hopping up and down, ordering Dad to hurry up with the house key.

I helped Sherrie out of the car. She stretched and took a deep breath—as deep as she could with a baby squirming around and crowding her insides.

"Thanks, Sugar," she said. Sherrie's voice was like honey, slow and sweet. She had a Texas accent generations deep. I figured even if we lived in Utah the rest of our lives, Sherrie would still sound like the South.

"It feels good to stretch my legs," she said, putting her hand on her cheek. "A long car ride sure makes a girl need to powder her nose. Hand me my purse, Sugar." I did, and Sherrie took out a little silver compact. It clicked open, and she dabbed her forehead and nose with a little pink puff. "Thank you, Sadie. I feel like a new woman!" She put the compact back in her purse, walked up to the front door and put her arm around Dad.

After my mom died, Dad spent the next few years looking out windows, sighing, with his arms dropping limp at his sides. When he met Sherrie, he started spending less time looking far away and more time smiling and sometimes even laughing. Dad loves Sherrie. Zuzu and I love Sherrie. Sherrie loves all of us. But sometimes at night, I take out the shoe box that has a picture of my mom in it, and most of the time, I still cry.

"Hurry, hurry, hurry!" shouted Zuzu as Dad fumbled with the house key. The door opened with a groan, and Zuzu was inside and up the stairs before anyone else could get across the threshold.

"I'm going to get the air mattress for Sherrie," said Dad. "There are two bedrooms upstairs and two downstairs. You and Zuzu have the upstairs rooms."

"I'm taking this one!" Zuzu shouted from the top of the stairs.

"Isn't this exciting?" Sherrie whispered in my ear. "I bet I know which room you're going to have. When your dad and I first saw the house, I thought, 'This room looks just like Sadie! We'll take it!'" She smiled. "Besides, it's your season, and I think sitting in that room, you'll look just like Jackie O."

Sherrie loved Jackie Kennedy Onassis. She sold Bonnie Mae cosmetics, and every time she did a makeover, the ultimate compliment she could give was that the "after" looked just like Jackie O. The thing is, they usually did. "Go on. I'll be up in a few minutes to see your new room."

Far-Far-Away Blue

Dad came back and took Sherrie to their room to set up the air mattress.

The downstairs had a front room—in houses this old, they're called parlors. There were two bedrooms, a kitchen, a bathroom and a formal dining room. One of the downstairs bedrooms belonged to Dad and Sherrie. The extra downstairs bedroom was to be made up as a nursery for the new baby until Grandma Brooks got too old and needed to move in.

The house smelled old—the good kind of old. I looked at the banister as I went up the stairs to find my new bedroom. Dents marked the shiny dark wood from years of use. It felt like the house had seen a million things and wanted to tell us about them with little marks that a person had to look closely to see.

When I got to the top of the stairs, Zuzu was already hanging up a kitten poster in one of the rooms, so I knew the other was mine. My room was painted a color I would call far-far-away blue, and at the far end of the room was a large window. As soon as I saw the window, I knew it was my first choice—no matter who drew the smaller pencil.

Outside the window swayed a large sycamore tree. Its peeling bark looked like a paint-by-number picture, and its branches stretched all the way to the window, tapping the old flowing glass panes. Past the tree was the street and beyond the street, the mountains.

I opened the window. It creaked and groaned like it hadn't moved in decades. A breath of spicy air from the canyons drifted in and swirled around the room. The smell reminded me of the good things that came with visiting Grandma Brooks. To me, it smelled like Grandma herself.

I turned and looked around. I touched the walls and window and wondered who had lived in the room before me. It felt lived in, like it was crammed full of history and stories. I wanted to know who had been here before. I wanted to know the history and stories of the room as I added my own.

The closet was deep and I went all the way to the back. It felt good to be in the dark where I could just feel the space with my breath. Zuzu would say I was being weird. Something crunched under my tennis shoe. I bent down and picked it up. It was a brass button with a scene of a Chinese pagoda and a crane with open wings. It looked like the kind of thing a person sees in a grandma's sewing basket. I felt like the room was welcoming me. I set the button on the windowsill so I could see it and remember.

"Sadie, sugar, you got a room yet?" called Sherrie from downstairs.

"Yeah."

"Can your dad and I come up and see it?"

"Sure." Their footsteps creaked up the stairs. The house sounded tired, like the stiff old bones in Dad's neck.

I didn't mind moving to Utah. Zuzu did. She had about a billion friends in Texas, and she threw tantrums every night for months when she found out we were leaving. I don't have a billion friends. I'm not as pretty as Zuzu. She looks a bit like Shirley Temple with her halo of golden curls and cherub face. She even has a dimple in each cheek. I don't have any dimples. Most people call me the smart one. I guess they

Far-Far-Away Blue

mean it as consolation for my not being pretty, but I don't mind. I know I'm smart, and I'd rather be smart than pretty. Pretty doesn't get you into gifted and talented classes where you get to read more advanced books and do more advanced art and all that. Zuzu has to sit in her boring regular classes looking beautiful. I don't think she minds.

I'm thin and I have straight brown hair that gets stringy if I don't wash it every day—and sometimes I don't. I have blue eyes like Zuzu's, but mine aren't framed with lush black lashes like hers. I have freckles that Sherrie calls adorable, and naturally straight teeth. I suppose those are my good points as far as looks are concerned. I'm not tall or short or anything out of the ordinary. I guess that is what you could call my looks—ordinary. I'm fine with it.

"I knew this was your room!" Sherrie said, clapping her hands in the doorway. "Norman, didn't I say this room was made for Sadie?"

"Yes, I believe you did," he said, looking out the window.

"This room just feels like you, Sadie, and that aqua blue is your season."

They walked out of the room and down the hall to Zuzu's. I heard Sherrie say, "Oh, I knew you'd pick this one! Sitting on your bed in here, you'll look just like Jackie O!"

Cave-Dwelling White

THE SECOND THING I REMEMBER, after hearing my story, is color. Grandma Brooks came to stay with Zuzu and me when my mom died. She brought yarn and spent her days tending us and crocheting. I remember the plain brown bag stuffed full with bright skeins of every-color yarn. Grandma read me the names of the colors and I remember them all.

She told Dad I was an artist because even though I was only four, I loved the colors and texture of the yarn and the sound of the color names. Grandma Brooks always bought Miss Vickie's Colorful Creations brand yarn. Miss Vickie must have been an artist, too, because the names were as vivid as the colors themselves. I remember Primeval Green, Judgment-Day White, Orange Smolder and Oh, So Noir. My new room in regular colors would be robin's-egg blue, because it looks like a robin's egg. In Miss Vickie's colors, it would be Far-Far-Away Blue. Zuzu's would be

Sugar-Punch Pink. I think Zuzu herself would be Sugar-Punch Pink.

Grandma Brooks bought me a set of watercolors in a tin box for my sixth birthday, and I've never been anywhere without a little paint set since.

If I see something wonderful or terrible, beautiful or hideous, funny or sad, I paint it so I can remember. I guess painting is my version of a diary.

I like to mix colors and give them Miss Vickie kind of names—the kind of names you smell, touch, taste and feel. I try to make names that remind me of what was happening when I made the color. For example, I made skinned-elbow red after I fell on the sidewalk and scraped my arm. I went home to paint what happened and the color just came to me.

I still remember the first thing I painted. It was the neighbor's puppy. I used roll-in-the-dirt brown and used-to-be white. It looked pretty good, if I do say so myself.

Before we left Houston, I packed my paints in my backpack—right at the top so I could get to them easily. I wanted to remember just what the house looked like before we put all of our stuff in it.

I took out my paints and the new pad of watercolor paper I had bought just for the move. I looked out the window. The moving van was pulling up to the curb. A few curious neighbors peeked out of doors and windows.

In the front yard, a girl who looked about my age stood waving. I watched her for a second before I realized she was waving at me. I pointed to myself and mouthed, "Me?" The girl nodded. I nodded back.

I closed the window and went outside to meet my new neighbor.

She had long, straight, freezing-cold black hair, the kind of black that's almost blue. Her eyes were deep honey-black, and her skin was very fair. "Fair" skin can sometimes mean a soft milky complexion or it can be a polite way to say pale and almost cave-dwelling white.

"Hi," I said. The girl didn't answer, but held out a fist. I looked at the closed hand. I didn't know if she was threatening me or what.

"Here," she said. I still didn't know what she meant, so I just stood there feeling confused. She opened her hand. On her palm lay a tear-shaped crystal. It looked like a diamond. "Here," she repeated.

"What? For me?"

"Yes," she said.

I took the crystal and examined it. It had a hole drilled in the top and looked like it was meant to be hung like a fancy costume necklace or something. It was kind of sticky and smelled like oranges.

"If you hang it in a window, it will make rainbows," she said.

"Thank you," I said. "It's beautiful. I'm Sadie Brooks. I'm thirteen."

"I'm Belladonna Desolation," the girl said, closing her eyes and turning her face to the sky. It looked like she was absorbing the sunshine. It looked like she could use some sunshine. "I'm thirteen, too."

"Oh," I said.

"I'll let you call me Bella." She paused for a second, returning her gaze to the crystal lying on my palm. Then she looked down at her feet. "If you want."

"Okay."

"Do you think I'm bold and mysterious?" Bella asked.

"What?"

"Do you think I'm bold and mysterious?"

I didn't know what the right answer was. I glanced at Bella's dress. It was old-fashioned, just-plain black, and so long, it pooled in the grass. It looked like a gown that a pioneer woman would wear—a depressed pioneer woman. She looked so sad, I figured she must be from the Great Dog. I guessed she wanted me to say yes.

"Uh, yes."

Bella smiled, then checked herself and instantly erased the happy expression. "Do you like cats?" she asked.

"Yeah, I guess. Do you?"

"Yes."

Bella scanned our yard intently. She bit her bottom lip and squinted. She looked like she was searching for the meaning of life in the sycamore tree. Then her eyes returned to me.

"If you look out your attic window, you can see the cemetery," Bella whispered. I didn't know there was a cemetery out the attic window. I didn't even know there was an attic or an attic window. Bella waited for some sort of response.

"A cemetery," I said.

"It's haunted. I go to my attic all the time and look out the window for ghosts."

"Have you seen any?"

"Maybe, well, no, well, I'm not sure, but I know I will sometime. Go to your attic tonight and see if you can see any ghosts out your window."

"Uh, okay. I'll try to get up there tonight to look." I stared at Bella, unsure what to think of her. Just then, a woman who looked like a pretend mom from a TV commercial, the kind that is always holding cupcakes or cool drinks or something, walked out onto the front porch of the house next door. She had bottle-blond hair in a perfect bob. She wore a cool-summer-white top and perfectly ironed pants. She even had an apron tied around her waist. I could almost imagine her saying something like she was in a commercial: "Mmmm, that's delicious. Pick up a glass today!"

"Kristin," she called.

Bella started to turn toward the voice, but stopped and turned back to me.

"Kristin. Come on, I need you to help me finish juicing these oranges so we can get them done for the church breakfast tomorrow."

Bella hesitated. She stood with her skirt pooling in the grass like she had no idea what to do, so I said, "Thanks for the beautiful crystal, Bella. Oh, and for the heads-up about the you-know-what out the attic window." Bella smiled in spite of herself. Her smile was beautiful and bright and took over her entire face. It almost had a color of its own. She looked at the ground and ran home, gathering up her black dress in her fists.

Royal-Jewels Red

GRANDMA BROOKS HUGGED ME SO tightly, it felt more like a wrestling hold than a hug.

"Thirteen!" she said, holding my shoulders at arm's length to get a good look at how I'd grown. "My, my, you're practically a woman!"

"Me, too, Grandma Brooks! How about me?" shouted Zuzu, hopping up and down in the doorway.

"Oh, my, I almost didn't recognize you," Grandma said, taking Zuzu by the shoulders. "You look so grown up, I think I might start calling you Susan." Zuzu's name really was Susan—Susan Lorraine Brooks. Everyone called her Zuzu because that's how I said Susan when she was born and it just kind of stuck.

"Hi, Mother," said Dad.

"How's my boy?" Grandma said, hugging him maybe even harder than she had hugged me. He didn't seem to mind.

"I'm doing fine. Thanks for having us over for dinner."

"Hi, Iona," said Sherrie.

"Would you look at this rose." Grandma Brooks touched Sherrie's protruding tummy tenderly. "You look like a perfect bloom." They smiled at each other and hugged. They both jumped and started laughing because they said the baby kicked and startled them both.

"Oh, before I forget," said Grandma Brooks, disappearing into the kitchen and returning with a package wrapped in silver paper. "Here you go—for the new home."

Sherrie tore the paper and pulled out an almost-nighttime-blue and just-plain-white crocheted box-shaped thing. "It's a toaster cozy," said Grandma. "Just pull the ribbon on the bottom and it will adjust to fit any toaster."

"Thanks, Iona," said Sherrie. She kissed Grandma Brooks on the cheek. "Won't this look nice in the kitchen, Norman?"

"Yes."

"I was going to crochet some matching hanging towels and dishrags," said Grandma. "But I thought I'd wait and see how you all fix up the place first."

"That would be real nice. Thank you," said Sherrie.

I loved Grandma Brooks' house. All the houses in the neighborhood were old. In Houston all the houses were new, with big rooms, big garages, and small yards. Old houses have tiny rooms, no garages and big backyards. Zuzu and I used to try to find secret hiding places at Grandma Brooks' house. It seems in houses like hers, there is always a space under the stairs, or behind some corner, or under something you wouldn't expect. Now we had our own old house with secret places to discover and explore.

Grandma showed everyone to the table that was spread with the good china. A huge sugary ham sizzled and steamed. A casserole of funeral potatoes with crushed cornflakes on the top sat next to a large bowl of salad. I knew there must be Jell-O setting in the fridge. Grandma Brooks' Jell-O was always royal-jewels red with little bits of canned oranges and lots of miniature marshmallows floating around inside. Life shifts around and flip-flops, but a person can always count on the comfortable feeling of things staying the same at Grandma's table.

After dinner, everyone got up to go to the parlor and visit—all except Zuzu, who had fallen asleep facedown at the table.

Before we even got there, Dad said, "It's been a long day, Mom. Do you mind if we just call it a night?"

"Of course I mind," she said, smiling, "but it looks like it's probably for the best."

Dad picked up Zuzu, who started talking softly in her sleep.

"It's not fair. Jennifer Meyer's mom lets her . . . Twinkies . . . ," she mumbled, and then she dropped her head on Dad's shoulder and started snoring contentedly. She was way too big to carry, but I guess Dad considered this an exception.

When good-byes and thank-yous and even more hugs were exchanged, we walked out into the night. It was darker than I expected. The wind blew down from the canyons, and it felt fresh and clean, like the new air sweeping away the old. Our house was only three doors down from Grandma's, but my body was so tired from the move, it felt much farther.

When we arrived at our house, Bella's front door opened. She looked at me and put her fingers to her lips like she was shushing me. She whispered something, but I couldn't understand her.

"What?" I mouthed.

"Remember—the attic!" Bella mouthed back. I nodded and went inside.

Fuzzy-Monster Green

I COULDN'T SLEEP. THE SYCAMORE scratched at the glass, and the house settled with strange cracks and pops. It was only ten o'clock, but everyone was in bed, and the sound of snoring added to the sounds of the mellowing house. I kicked the covers one way, then the next. My legs twitched restlessly and I tensed my body and relaxed it, hoping it would help me sleep. It didn't. I thought of Bella and the teardrop glass piece. I tossed off the covers and put on my fuzzy-monster-green slippers. I decided to find the attic.

Since nearly everything was still taped up tight in boxes, I couldn't find my flashlight, so I decided to just try to see by moonlight. I realized it was a dumb idea when I banged right into my closed bedroom door.

The staircase to the downstairs was beautiful polished dark wood—like it had been designed to be seen. The one to the attic was narrow, plain and tucked out of the way—like it had been designed to be hidden. I felt my way up the stairs and opened the door at the top.

The attic sprawled into one enormous room that covered the entire story. It smelled like old. I hoped there weren't any spiders. I hated spiders. The room was too dark to see many details, but I did find four small windows—each pitched to a little gable on each side of the room. The glass in each window flowed and rippled and made the outside look kind of wavy. Gables were pointed like little triangles over each window. The roof ridge was the high point of the room, and the rest of the room sloped down from there.

The window to the south looked over the front yard like my bedroom window. The one to the west looked over neighbors' houses, and I could see Grandma Brooks' house—or at least her roof. From the window on the east I could look right into Bella's house, which was just as dark as ours. To the north, I saw the backyard and blackness.

I pulled up a wooden crate and placed it in front of the north window. I sat down and squinted to try to see anything at all. As my eyes adjusted to the darkness, I began to make out vague shapes. Over the houses behind ours, I saw the outlines of gravestones. Nighttime made them almost invisible, and if I hadn't known what I was looking for, I'd probably have missed them entirely.

I heard little, tiny ticking and popping sounds that I was sure I'd never be able to hear in the daytime. Suddenly, the hair on my arms rose and prickled. The night felt almost heavy and solid, like an actual presence. The darkness wrapped around me like fingers, getting tighter and tighter. I wanted

Fuzzy-Monster Green

to turn away and run back to my bed, but something made me want to look harder out the window and see if the ghosts were real. At that moment, it felt absolutely possible.

My heart thumped wildly in my chest. The thumping seemed so loud, I was sure it would wake everyone in the house. Gripping the box underneath me, my fingernails dug into the rough wood. A large splinter jammed itself under my nail and I jumped. I crammed the stinging finger into my mouth and tasted blood. It was too dark to see the blood or the splinter.

I looked over to the window facing Bella's house and jumped so high, I tumbled off the box. Bella stood at her attic window, holding a candle and looking directly at me. I gasped and tried to orient myself in the dark. My chest was so tight, I had to grab for breath trying to find which way was up in the thick blackness. Stumbling across the floor and darting down the stairs, I returned to my room. I shut the curtains and climbed into bed, pulling the covers up over my head, and stayed like that the whole night.

Lavender Despair

SUNLIGHT FILTERED THROUGH THE closed curtains, making my room look even more far-far-away blue. I woke up stiff and tired from a night of half vigilance. The covers lay over my face and I could hardly breathe. Sweaty hair clung to my skin and my finger throbbed. There was a large splinter under the nail. In the sunlight, it was easy to take out. Trudging downstairs, I scratched my head trying to untangle my damp hair.

Zuzu and Dad sat at the kitchen table with plates of un-eaten toast in front of them. The clock said nine-fifteen, and Zuzu was already throwing a tantrum.

"Why can't I go, too? You never take me anywhere fun! How come Sadie gets to do all the fun stuff and I have to stay home and do all the work?"

"Sadie's going to stay here and watch you, and anyway, it's only for a few hours," said Dad between sips of coffee.

"Jennifer Meyer's mom lets her go everywhere with her! She knows how to treat a child!"

"Zuzu, please. Eat your toast."

"What's going on?" I asked, taking a seat by Dad.

"Sherrie and I are going to the appliance store to see if we can get the dishwasher replaced. This one's too small for our family and it's pretty worn out."

"Jeez, Zuzu, all the screaming for that?" I said. "Sounds pretty boring to me." Zuzu stuck her tongue out at me.

"That'll do, girls," said Dad. "After we order the dishwasher, Sherrie and I are going out for lunch downtown with Grandma Brooks."

"How could she not invite us?" wailed Zuzu. "What if we starve while you and Sherrie are running around at fancy restaurants? What if you come back and find our bodies, wasted away? How would you feel then?"

"He'd probably wish he'd stuck with the smaller dishwasher," I said.

"You're not funny, Sadie! You think you are, but you're not!" Zuzu threw down her napkin and dashed upstairs.

"Sorry to leave you with Zuzu. She seems off this morning," said Dad, picking up his plate and loading it in the too-small dishwasher.

"Yeah, 'off,'" I said, rolling my eyes. We heard Zuzu's muffled shouting from upstairs.

"I'm packing my suitcase now! I've had enough of this family! I'm tired of being the slave—starved, overworked, not appreciated! When you get home, I'll be on my way to Houston!

I'm sure Jennifer Meyer's mom would take me in any day, and I'm sure she'll always let me come to restaurants with her!"

I was pouring a bowl of Frosty Cocoa Flakes when Sherrie came in the front door. She had about a million bags in her hands, so Dad jumped up to help her.

"Thanks, Norman," she said. She sat down in a chair and breathed heavily. When she realized I was watching her, she pretended she wasn't out of breath and that she was ready to climb a mountain. She never wanted people to feel sorry for her. She never wanted to appear like she was slowing down or needed help.

"Sadie, you're gonna love what I got!" she said. She pushed herself out of the chair with her arms and opened one of the bags. "I got you this book. It's called *Mimi Jones, Clever Girl Detective—The Case of the Missing Opal*. I thought of you right away."

Sherrie thinks I am the smartest girl in the world—at least that's what she says. Whenever she sees anything that has to do with intelligent girls—especially books—she gets it for me. I suppose she thinks I can relate to it if it has to do with smarts. To tell the truth, I'm not always crazy about the things she gets me, but I love the thought so much that I usually end up liking them anyway.

"Thank you, Sherrie," I said, and I kissed her on the cheek.

"Also," she said, winking at me, "I found this little handbag that was so cute I had to buy one for Zuzu." She pulled a tiny plastic sugar-punch-pink purse out of the bag and handed it to me. A huge school-glue-white flower on the front seemed to burst and bloom right out of some polka-dot garden. She headed upstairs to give it to Zuzu. Sherrie always knew exactly what she was doing. Once Zuzu saw the purse, she'd be so enraptured, she'd forget all about the tragic injustices she suffers at the hands of the Brooks family and behave the rest of the afternoon.

Someone knocked on the door. I answered it. Bella stood on the front porch holding a large cardboard box.

"Did you see any?" she said.

"Any what?" I asked.

"Ghosts."

"No."

"Me neither. I thought I did for a second, but I think it must have been a bird or something. I'm going to try again tonight. I brought you something."

I invited her in. Bella glanced around the living room with a look like she had just stepped into a cave—taking in every detail and scanning for danger. She set the box on the floor and sat down beside it. I followed.

"My cat Lavender Despair had babies," Bella said. She opened the box to reveal three tiny kittens. They mewed and squirmed and looked so cute I could hardly resist picking one up. "They're eight weeks old and we have to give them away. I named them all." She put her hand in the box and the kittens swarmed around her fingers, batting and purring. "I call that black one Raven Badfire," she said. "And this gray one Calamity." She handed me the foggy-morning-colored kitten. It curled up in my hands and chewed playfully on my fingers. "The white one I call Ivory Abyss."

"They are so cute!" I said, picking up Raven Badfire. The kitten's tiny claws dug into my shirt. It climbed up to my shoulder and mewed in my ear. It tickled. Bella placed Ivory Abyss in my arms, and when Dad walked into the room, I was covered with the mewing bundles.

"Can you keep one?" asked Bella.

"What? You mean have one of your kittens?" I said.

"Yes."

I looked at my dad.

"Well, I don't know . . ." He was interrupted by a shriek as Zuzu darted into the room.

"Kittens!" she shouted. "Can we keep them? Please! Please! Please!"

"Well, I don't know," Dad repeated.

"Please, Daddy! I'll wash the dishes every day for a year—two years!" shouted Zuzu. "I'll clean the bathrooms and sweep the stairs! Please!"

"I'll have to talk to Sherrie," said Dad. Just then Sherrie walked into the room.

"Oh!" she said. "How adorable!" She walked over to us and sat down on the floor.

"I'm Belladonna Desolation," said Bella. She looked at Sherrie like she was scanning for some sort of reaction.

"Oh," said Sherrie, "uh, I'm Sherrie. Pleased to make your acquaintance, Ms. Desolation. You must hear this all the time, but you have lovely, smoky-mysterious eyes." Sherrie held out her hand and smiled. She always knew how to compliment people. She always meant the compliments, too. Whatever reaction Bella was looking for, she must have found it, because she smiled as she shook Sherrie's hand. It was a shy smile, like she was embarrassed to have someone paying attention to her. When I'd first met her, I'd seen the sad look in her eyes and thought she was from the Great Dog, but now I thought different. She was so bashful, I decided she must be from Adam and Eve. Bella peeled one of the kittens from my shirt and placed it in Sherrie's hands.

"Her name is Calamity," said Bella. "Do you want her? She's my favorite and we have to give her away."

"Oh, she's so soft!" said Sherrie. "Hello, little Calamity, hello, you're so cute. Yes, you are. Yes, you are," she said in a coochy-coochy-coo voice. After a minute, Sherrie looked up at Dad. He shrugged, rolled his eyes and walked into the other room.

"Sadie," Sherrie said, putting the kitten in her lap. It immediately scaled her round belly and curled up on the top. "Well, you are thirteen years old and practically a woman. I got the first pet that was my very own when I was thirteen. Could you be responsible for her?"

"Yes!" I exclaimed, sounding almost like Zuzu.

"Hey!" shouted Zuzu. "I'm responsible, too!"

"Yes, Zuzu. Maybe when you're thirteen, we can discuss a pet for you, too," said Sherrie. "Sadie, a kitten is a big responsibility."

"I know," I said.

"And they don't stay kittens forever."

"This family is so MEAN!" Zuzu shouted, stamping her Sunday shoes in the wooden floor.

"I know they don't," I said.

"You'd have to feed her and change her litter box."

"I will."

Sherrie stroked the kitten, lifted it off her stomach and handed it to me. "You know, having a pet can actually reduce the look of aging," she said. "Not that y'all need that yet, but attention to proper rejuvenation can never start too soon. Calamity, welcome to our home."

"Thank you!" I shouted.

"NO FAIR!" hollered Zuzu. She ran out of the room and up the stairs, and slammed her bedroom door. Sherrie kissed the top of my head and went off to the kitchen.

"I saw you last night," said Bella. Her words brought my heart back up into my throat.

"Yeah, you scared the daylights out of me."

"Oh, sorry. Want me to show you the cemetery? I mean show you out your attic window."

"Okay."

We placed Calamity back in the box and went to the attic. Bella walked in like it was her own house and headed straight for the north window. She picked up the toppled wooden crate and sat down.

The attic looked totally different during the day. It was full of old boxes and crates—like someone decades and decades ago had packed up to go, but changed their mind. Everything was dusty, and it smelled kind of like a museum. With the ceiling and walls at sloping angles and the boxes and crates scattered here and there, it looked like there were little hidden corners all over the large room. I knew that, besides my bedroom, this was going to be my favorite room of the house.

"There," she said, pointing straight ahead. "I look for ghosts all the time—at least twice a week."

"Oh," I said, squinting out the window.

"I read in a book once that twenty-five percent of the people you see walking down the street on any given day are really just spirits." She scanned the cemetery with her honey-black eyes. "See that lady with all the kids?"

On the sidewalk near the cemetery, a woman was pushing a stroller surrounded by three small children, jumping around her like puppies.

"Yeah," I said.

"If the book is correct, one of those people is a spirit. Which one do you think?"

"I . . . I don't know." I didn't know what to make of this ghost talk. I wasn't even sure I believed in ghosts, let alone that twenty-five percent of people walking down the street were spirits. I didn't want to hurt Bella's feelings, so I picked one. "That one with the red sweater and braids, I guess," I said, pointing to a little girl who was sucking her thumb and looking up at the sky.

"I think so, too," said Bella.

"How come?" I said.

"Because the lady is Mrs. Hunter and two of those kids are hers, but not that one."

"Maybe she's babysitting," I said.

"Babysitting!?" said Bella, turning to me. "That's crazy!

She's a friend of my older sister, and I know for a fact she hates watching other people's kids!"

Bella pulled a small zebra-striped notebook from the folds of her skirt. "Little girl with Mrs. Hunter . . . ," she mumbled as she scribbled in the notebook.

"What's that?" I asked, leaning over the tiny pages.

"Data," said Bella. "I record every possible ghost sighting I have in here. Someday I am going to write a book. Are you shocked?"

"Yes," I said. "Very."

She turned and looked at me and let out a sound that was almost a giggle. I did, too. I stepped away from the window to find another wooden crate to sit on.

"What kind of book?" I asked, heading toward a stack of about a dozen crates that sat in a corner of the attic. I chose one that looked the least likely to have spiders in it or cause splinters.

"A book about everyday ghosts and how to spot them, or something like that. I haven't nailed it down all the way yet."

"Sounds interesti . . ." I moved the probably spiderless crate and saw something. I pushed a few of the other crates away. "Bella," I said.

"Uh-huh?" she said, burying the notebook back in her skirts.

"Come here."

Bella knelt down next to me on the dusty attic floor.

"Whoa!" we said in unison. Behind the crates lay a crawl space. It looked like the crates had been arranged purposely to hide it. We peeked inside. It was dark and hard to see.

"I'll be right back," I said. That morning, I had remembered which box held my flashlight. I ran to my room and fumbled through the box until I found it. I raced back up the stairs.

When I turned the light on, we both gasped. The space was small, but just big enough for Bella and me and maybe one other person—a small person. We crawled inside.

On the inside, arched over the doorway, were the hand-painted words *Palace Beautiful*.

"What do you suppose it means?" Bella asked.

"I don't know."

I moved the flashlight around the tiny room. The space was almost square, maybe five feet deep by six feet long. It wasn't tall enough to stand up, and the ceiling slanted a bit and was lower the farther it lay from the opening. The walls were made of thick plank boards and exposed wall beams. The floor was rough, unfinished wood.

In one corner of the space, a candle in a tin candleholder sat in a pool of dusty, hardened wax. Just over the candle hung an old black-and-white photograph. It was a picture of a family—a mom, dad, three girls and a baby. A necklace was draped from the same nail that held the photo. It was a simple silver chain so old that it was muddy-black. A pearl circled with little diamonds dangled from the chain. I touched the pearl and set it swinging back and forth like the pendulum on a clock. I guessed it was the first time it had moved in decades.

On the wall opposite the candle, a beat-up book lay tucked between two wall beams. I picked it up. It had a butterfly-wing-blue cover with the word *Journal* printed in gold letters.

Someone had scribbled a note on the inside cover of the book. It said,

> To whoever finds this journal,
>
> I'm leaving this book behind on purpose. All the bad things in the world lie inked on these pages, and at the present, I don't want to remember.
>
> Sincerely,
>
> Helen White

"Open it!" Bella ordered excitedly. I did. I fanned the yellowing pages. The book was just over half full of handwritten journal entries.

"Oh, let's read it!" said Bella, almost not breathing.

Just then, Zuzu poked her head in the doorway of the little room. Bella and I both jumped.

"What are you doing?" Zuzu asked.

"We found this little room and there's an old journal! We're going to read it!" said Bella.

"Bella! Why did you tell her?" I said, almost shouting.

"I—I didn't know we weren't telling."

"Well, we weren't!"

"Hey!" shouted Zuzu.

"Sorry." Bella looked at her feet. Her face fell and she looked like a kicked puppy. I felt bad for hurting her feelings, but at the same time, I had no intention of including Zuzu. Bella's bottom lip quivered, and I knew I'd gone too far.

"I'm sorry, Bella," I said, looking at my own feet like I'd come from Adam and Eve or something.

"That's all right," she said. "I just don't see why she can't know about it. It's her house, too."

"That's right," Zuzu insisted. "It's my house, too!" Zuzu looked at me with an eagerness that surpassed any eagerness I'd seen in her before. I sighed.

"Can you keep a secret?" I asked.

"Yes!"

"Do you promise?"

"I promise I'll keep it a secret," said Zuzu. "Please?"

"Do you swear?"

Zuzu's eyes widened and she put her hand on her heart. "I swear! I'll be your slave or servant or maid or anything you want!" Her whole body tensed with anticipation.

"We don't need a maid or a servant," said Bella.

"Besides, she'd never clean up anyway. She's only good at one thing—throwing tantrums," I said. I knew it was over the line as soon as I said it, but I didn't apologize.

"Hey!" said Zuzu. "I'm telling!" Instinctively, she turned to leave, but she caught herself.

Bella shrugged. I sighed. I knew it was too late to say no. She had already seen the room.

"Well, all right, come on in. But you can't be a baby in here," I said.

"Oh, thank you! Thank you! Thank you!" shrieked Zuzu, flinging her arms around my neck and kissing me on the cheek. She repeated the process with Bella. Bella blushed and looked surprised and delighted by the show of affection.

"Wait!" said Zuzu. "We're forgetting someone!" She dashed out the doorway.

"No one else, Zuzu, you promised!" I called, but it was too late.

A moment later, she came back cradling Calamity in her arms. I smiled. Maybe I was selling her short.

Calamity padded around until she found my lap. She curled up and went to sleep purring.

"Let's read the first entry," I said. "Then we can read a few entries every day. That way we can spread it out longer."

"Oh, why can't we just read the whole thing?" whined Zuzu. She looked at us and then checked herself. "I mean, that sounds good."

We all nodded to each other and Bella took the book in her hands. She opened it to the first entry.

September 26, 1918

Today is my thirteenth birthday. It's been a wonderful day!

Mother made a cake with powdered sugar sprinkled on top. While the cake was cooling, Mother, Lizzy, Rachel and I went to the garden to pull weeds. Anna was still inside. We thought she was asleep in the parlor, well, she wasn't. When we came back inside, the cake was torn to bits and almost half eaten. We found Anna hiding under the kitchen table. We asked her if she had eaten the cake and she said no. Mother set her on a chair and asked her who had eaten it then. Anna still denied she had had anything to do with it even though she was covered with crumbs and powdered sugar. When Mother asked a third time who had eaten the cake, Anna said, "Woodrow

Wilson." We all laughed so hard that Anna started to say, "Woodrow Wilson, Woodrow Wilson, Woodrow Wilson . . ." over and over. Father had said just the other day that the war and politics were creeping into the family home. I guess he was right. Little Anna is just two and a half years old and already she knows the president.

Since this is my first entry, I think I should introduce myself and my family. My father's name is Samuel Walter White. He works as a lawyer at Denton and White in downtown Salt Lake City. My mother's name is Elizabeth Baker White. My father and mother married on October 11, 1902.

My sister Elizabeth was born the next year. We call her Lizzy. She is almost fifteen and she knows just about everything—at least she thinks she does. Not quite two years later, in 1905, I was born. The next year, the twins Thomas and Joseph were born, but they died before they were a month old. I don't remember them. After the twins died, Mother was sick for a long time and Aunt Margaret came to stay with us while Mother recovered. About a year and a half after the twins died, my sister Rachel was born. She was a sweet, quiet baby and she is still just as sweet and quiet. In 1911, my brother Edward was born, but he died when he was six months old. I helped make his little white burial gown. He was such a sweet little brother I almost couldn't bear it when he died. Finally, two and a half years ago, Anna was born. She was born on December 24 of 1915—our Christmas present.

Mother is currently awaiting a blessed event. Father would love to have a son. He never says so, but we know he would. Each time Mother has received a boy, the baby has died. I am afraid that if we have a brother, we will lose him like we did the others. I am determined not to get attached to the baby if it should be a boy. If it is a girl, I want Mother and Father to name her Frances. Lizzy wants to name her Eva, but Rose Taylor's little sister is named Eva and she pushed Anna into the mud after church. She said it was an accident, but I know it was on purpose, so I hope we name the baby Frances. That is our family so far.

This evening for dinner Mother made my favorite— chicken stew and biscuits. We had the first green apples of the season with what was left of the cake for dessert. Lizzy gave me a beautiful hair comb she bought with her pocket money. She must have seen me eyeing it in the shop window. I have it on right now. Rachel gave me a sewing roll. She made it herself out of scraps from the ragbag. The roll has four pockets—one for thread, one for needles and pins, one for a thimble and one for my tiny pair of embroidery scissors. I love it! Rachel is always so gentle and thoughtful. She always knows just what to do for people.

Anna gave me a big hug and a sloppy, wet kiss. She tried to give me her doll Millie, but I wouldn't take it. I'm sure she was relieved. Father and Mother gave me this journal and a pen. I am so excited to have my own little book to write in.

I have to go help Mother get Anna ready for bed now.
It was a wonderful birthday!
    —Helen

"Wow!" said Zuzu when I closed the book. "She lived here in this house! I wonder which room was hers."

"This one," said Bella, touching the raw wooden structure beams.

"This couldn't have been her bedroom," I said. "It was hiding behind old crates that look like they have been here forever. This was her secret room."

"Let's have this be our secret room!" said Zuzu.

"Let's!" said Bella, clapping her hands like a five-year-old on Christmas morning.

"We have to have some rules," I said. "Like no one can read the journal without the other two."

"Deal!" said Zuzu and Bella in unison.

"And we can't tell anybody about it—Zuzu!"

"Hey! I never tell secrets!" Zuzu punched her fists into her hips and frowned.

"Yes you do!"

"Not important ones!"

"I think we should call this place something," said Bella, picking up Calamity and stroking her baby-soft fur.

"What?" asked Zuzu.

"How about Palace Beautiful?" she said, pointing to the painted letters over the door. The name sounded ridiculously grand for this dusty old attic corner, but at the same time, somehow it fit perfectly.

"Perfect!" I said.

"Sadie," came a call from downstairs. We all—even Calamity—jumped and climbed out of Palace Beautiful. We stacked the crates back in front of the little doorway and ran down the attic steps. When we got to the main stairway, we walked down like nothing had happened and we had just been hanging out in my room or something.

"We're leaving, girls," said Sherrie.

"Bye," said Dad. "We'll see you in a couple of hours."

Just as Dad put his hand on the doorknob to leave, someone knocked on the other side. He opened the door.

"Hi, I'm Holly Smith," said the TV commercial mom from the day before. "I've been meaning to come over and introduce myself. I live next door. Here is some homemade bread. I always think a house feels like a home when it smells like fresh bread." She spoke nervously and fluttery, like a little bird and not at all like a lady on a commercial. Her eyes darted and flicked from the house to all of us and back again.

"Thank you, Holly," said Sherrie. "I'm Sherrie Brooks and this is my husband, Norman. You've probably seen the girls Sadie and Zuzu in the yard."

"Yes, my daughter has had the pleasure of meeting Sadie, and if Zuzu's the adorable little angel with the blond curls, I've seen her, too."

I snickered at the "angel" bit and Zuzu elbowed me in the ribs.

"I was wondering if Kristin is here by any chance?" Holly asked.

"Uh, I'm sorry, I'm not sure I know a Kristin," said Sherrie.

"I'm here," said Bella, walking to the door with the box cradled in her arms.

"Oh," said Sherrie. "I guess we *do* know a Kristin, only we call her Bella."

Bella beamed, looked at the floor and blushed. Holly blushed, too—a different kind of blush, though. She looked like I felt one time at school when my skirt was tucked into my underwear and I didn't know it until someone told me in the lunch line. She looked beyond regular embarrassed.

"They chose Calamity," said Bella.

Holly laughed uncomfortably. "Calamity, huh?" she said, partly to Bella and partly to us. "You have a way with words, Dear. I was calling that kitten Missy."

Bella stared at her mom with a look of utter disgust. "Who would name any kitten anything so awful?" she said in a tone almost as earnest as Zuzu's.

"Well, it was nice to meet you all," said Holly, trying to shuffle Bella out the door.

"Thanks for the bread," Sherrie called.

"Mom, can I stay? Please?" Bella asked.

"No, you most certainly cannot."

"Can I come back later?"

"Not today. Now stop that whining, Kristin. You know how I feel about whining." Holly reached up and pushed a strand of perfect hair that had become unperfected out of her eyes. She smiled. Her smile looked just like Miss America's. "Thanks again for having her over, and welcome to the neighborhood."

"Our door's always open," said Sherrie. "Oh, I'm having a little Bonnie Mae get-together tomorrow night. If you and Bella want to come, we'd be delighted to have y'all."

"Thank you so much. I'll check my calendar," said Holly.

"Bye!" Bella said as she marched behind her mom across the yard with the box of kittens in her arms.

Dad and Sherrie left, too. I stepped out into the front yard and watched the car pull out of the driveway. The grass felt cool on my bare feet and the breeze ruffled my hair. Enormous white clouds were piled on top of the mountains, and from every direction I heard birds. I thought of my new kitten and Palace Beautiful and Bella, and for a moment, I forgot to miss Texas.

I went back inside to make a place in my room for Calamity.

Dusty-Old Brown, Dusty-Old Blue, Dusty-Old Red

"I'M TELLING SHERRIE YOU'RE DOING that," said Zuzu, standing in my bedroom doorway. She crossed her arms and planted her feet hard against the wooden floorboards.

"Doing what?" I said.

"Oh, you know!"

"No, I don't."

"That!" She pointed to the box I was stuffing with towels for the kitten.

"What?"

"Good towels?" she said, raising her eyebrows and putting her hands on her hips like she was saying the most logical thing in the world and I was too stupid to comprehend it.

"What are you talking about?" I said.

"Those are Sherrie's good towels you're putting in that box. She'll be so mad at you for letting a cat sleep on her good towels!"

"She said I could use them," I said.

"FINE!" Zuzu shouted. She stomped out the doorway, back into her room, and slammed the door.

I gathered up Calamity and placed her gently in the box. She mewed and picked at the cheek-rouge-pink towels with her tiny claws.

"There you go. I hope you like it," I said. I put the box on the floor by my bed and opened the window so she could have some fresh air.

I took out my paints and went to the attic. I wanted to paint Palace Beautiful the way it looked the day I found it.

After moving the crates from the little doorway, I climbed in and set my paints on the floor. Using my broadest brush and dullest colors, like dusty-old brown, dusty-old blue and dusty-old red, I began to paint. Looking at the room through the eyes of my paints, I thought it could use a bit more color, but it looked beautiful in its old and creaky way. There are always way more colors in a place than people usually notice anyway. The little room was filled with them, and imagining a girl my age up here writing in her journal gave it extra color and light. Touching the letters over the doorway, I wondered if she wrote them and what they meant. I brushed the words *Palace Beautiful* on the sheet of watercolor paper and blew on them softly so they would soak into the paper and become part of it. I painted every little detail I could find, from the necklace to the individual drips of the old candle. Painting makes a person look closer than they ever would normally. It makes them breathe and smell and touch and be a part of what they are painting. It makes time stop and something else begin. I don't know how

Dusty-Old Brown, Dusty-Old Blue, Dusty-Old Red

long I was in the little room, but when I was done, I knew every inch of the space and it felt like part of me.

Leaving the painting to dry in Palace Beautiful, I went to the north window. Cloud shadows passed over the cemetery, making it dark then light then dark again. I wondered who was buried in those graves. My skin itched and pricked with goose bumps. Was Helen White buried in that graveyard? If she was, did she haunt her little Palace in the attic? Closing my eyes, I asked the air, "Is anyone here?" All I heard was a puff of breeze pulling on the branches of an old knotty apple tree in the backyard. I asked again, "Is anyone here?" I tried to listen with my eyes, nose and mouth. My skin puckered with waves of goose bumps, and I wasn't sure whether they came as a sign from the other side or from just being creeped out in an attic. Either way, I didn't want to think about it anymore. So I went downstairs to make lunch.

I fixed two peanut butter and strawberry jam sandwiches out of the bread Bella's mom had made and called Zuzu to lunch. We took our sandwiches and a couple of apples into the backyard and had a picnic.

Zuzu was quiet. She bit into her sandwich and chewed absently. After a few minutes I saw a tear roll down her cheek.

"What's wrong?" I asked.

She didn't answer right away. I expected a sudden tantrum explosion, but instead, Zuzu looked up at me and said, "I was going to be lunchroom monitor next year." More fat tears dropped down her morning-rose-pink cheeks.

These weren't her usual trying-to-get-her-way tears, these

were tears of real pain. In all the craziness of moving, I'd almost forgotten to look back. I swallowed hard. I thought of my favorite sitting place by the bayou. I thought of my old school where I knew every hallway and just about every class-room. I thought about the big mall downtown where Sherrie would take us and let us spray ourselves with fancy perfume. I thought of Bluebell ice cream. I knew they wouldn't have it in Utah. If I hadn't been the babysitter for the afternoon, I would have cried, too.

"Maybe at your new school they'll need a lunchroom mon-itor," I said, but I knew good and well it wasn't the same.

"Maybe," she said. We ate the rest of our lunch in silence. The boiling-white clouds turned calamity-gray, then better-get-inside black. I remembered from visiting Grandma Brooks that afternoon storms popped up and disappeared often this time of year. It looked like we were about to get our first one. The breeze changed from warm to cool almost instantly. Thunder rumbled from somewhere, but it must have been far away because we didn't see any lightning.

Ancient-World White

THAT EVENING DAD INSTALLED THE new dishwasher, and Sherrie, Zuzu and I unpacked as many boxes as we could. The movers had done the big work of putting big things where they went, but we were doing the work that made it home. Sherrie even put the silver candlesticks on the dining room table. We get those out only for special occasions, but Sherrie said a new home is a special occasion.

When Sherrie lay down for a rest, I unpacked nearly all the boxes in my room and it started to really feel like mine. I read in a book once where a girl made friends with an apple tree outside her bedroom window. She even gave it a name. Zuzu would make fun of me if I gave the sycamore tree a name, but I decided that, as long as no one knew about it, the tree and I would be friends. I opened my window wide and reached out my arm. I stroked one of the fat velvety leaves and smiled. Calamity came up behind me and rubbed against my foot. My room was my room, and it was filled with soft things that made it home.

For dinner Dad said he was going to get some chicken and asked if I wanted to go with him.

"What do you think of the house?" he asked as we pulled out of the driveway.

"I like it."

"Do you miss Texas?"

I thought for a minute. "Yes," I said. We drove down South Temple Street. We passed a huge cathedral with gargoyles and everything. It looked haunted, and I thought Bella might like it there. "Yes, I miss Texas, but I like it here."

"Good," Dad said. He adjusted his hands on the steering wheel.

"Sherrie says you girls are a big help." An enormous stone mansion flashed past my window. "That's the governor's mansion," he said, pointing to a gas station. "Oh, I guess we passed it already. Anyway, thanks, Sadie. Thanks for making this a smoother transition for Sherrie."

"You're welcome."

My dad reminded me of a tree—always present, steady and strong, but silent and still. A person has to notice the tree. It's not going to make a big deal fussing over a person. It will just quietly make a shady spot and keep it there day after day until someone needs it. I loved my dad. He loved me. I understood him and I felt he understood me.

"Dad," I said, staring out the window. "How is . . . how does . . . is Sherrie all right?"

"What do you mean?" he asked.

"I mean, you know, the baby, moving to a new place, things being different. Is Sherrie all right with the baby?"

I didn't like to think about the baby. Moving had kept me so busy, I'd almost forgotten that Sherrie was pregnant at all. I almost felt afraid to forget. I wasn't thinking anything could go wrong when my mother had Zuzu, and that was when she died—when I forgot.

"Your mom," he started. He almost never talked about my mother. I could see pain behind his eyes whenever she was brought up. He still loved her. He loved Sherrie, too. I guess some circumstances called for extra space inside a person for loving several people 100 percent. "Your mom knew she was going to have complications when Zuzu was born."

"What do you mean?"

"I mean, she had trouble in childbirth with you, and the doctors told her she shouldn't have another baby."

"I didn't know that." I felt like my body had left the car and was hovering over some scene from years and years ago. I saw my mom with a swollen belly like Sherrie's. I saw for the first time that she knew. She knew what was going to happen. The doctor knew, Dad knew. The only ones who didn't know were Zuzu and me.

"Yeah, she almost died with you."

I looked back out my window. The Mormon temple stood out in the center of the city like an ancient-world-white European cathedral. I'd never seen another building like it. My throat tightened as I thought of my mom almost dying to bring me into the world. I didn't want to cry in front of my dad, but I felt like it.

"When we found out we were going to have Zuzu, we both had a feeling. . . ." He stopped and swallowed. "We knew what it could mean. Then one night, about two months before Zuzu was born, your mother had a dream that she was in a big room filled with light. She was with her parents and their parents and other people she loved. She looked out the doorway of the room and saw you two girls happy, strong and growing into 'fine young women,' as she put it. She also saw me with a woman at my side. Your mother said when she woke up that she knew she was going to die and that I would remarry and it would be best for our family."

I couldn't help it anymore. Tears ran down my cheeks.

"Has Sherrie . . . ," I started. "Has Sherrie had any dreams?"

"No," Dad answered.

I wondered if she had dreams that she just didn't tell him— dreams about dying. I thought of the thousands of dreams I've had and never told anyone. "Are you sure?"

We pulled into the Bubba's Southern Fried Chicken parking lot. Dad didn't pull up to the drive-through, though. He parked the car and turned to me. "Yes," he said. "Your mother and I knew she might die. Things are different with Sherrie. The doctor says she is strong and healthy. She's going to be fine. I don't want you to worry. I can understand why you'd be scared, and I won't say I haven't had the same fears, but things are different this time." He looked into my eyes so deeply and so kindly, I almost forgot to worry.

"Are you really sure?"

He took my hand and squeezed it. "Nothing in life is certain, Sadie, but I can tell you, this is different from your mother. It just is." He hugged me. I held on tight. I wanted

Ancient-World White

to believe him, and I tried with everything inside me. But wanting to believe and actually believing are two different things.

Dad started the car and we pulled up to the drive-through. I tried to smile at him to let him know I wasn't worried, but how could I not be worried? What if, once again, everyone knew something except Zuzu and me?

Wide-Awake Red

BELLA CAME OVER BEFORE I WAS EVEN out of bed the next morning. She came into my room and blushed to find me just waking up.

"Sorry," Bella said. "I guess I was anxious to read the journal."

I got out of bed and we went to Zuzu's room to wake her. Calamity followed, nipping and batting at my fuzzy-monster-green slippers.

Zuzu was awake—kind of. She sat up in bed when we walked in. She looked confused. Her hair was sticking up all over the place and she scratched at it.

"Come on, let's go to the attic," I said. She instantly woke up the rest of the way. She tossed off her covers, picked up Calamity and followed us up the stairs.

We pushed away the wooden crates hiding the tiny doorway.

"Wait!" said Zuzu. She pulled a piece of watercolor paper from behind one of the crates and held it up.

"Hey! I painted that!" I said, grabbing for the picture of Palace Beautiful.

"Before," said Zuzu.

"What?"

"After," she said, pulling away the last crate.

"Whoa!" Bella and I said.

The little crawl space was spotless. Zuzu had cleaned every surface. A rose-velvet-red-and-cumulous-white quilt was spread over the raw wood floor, and along the tops of the walls Zuzu had strung little clear Christmas lights. A camping lantern hung from the center of the room. It looked beautiful!

"You're welcome," said Zuzu, folding her arms and smiling.

"When did you do this?" I asked, still stunned.

"When you weren't looking. Come on in," said Zuzu, crawling in first.

"Look!" said Bella, tucking her floor-length black-black skirt under her knees and pointing to the corner of the room. The journal lay in a shoe box that was covered with ribbons and sparkles and painted with what looked like wide-awake-red nail polish.

"I thought it deserved a place of honor, so I made one for it," said Zuzu.

"I love it!" shouted Bella, flinging out her arms and whacking the camping lantern.

"And look," said Zuzu. She pointed to the doorway. She had made a curtain door by tacking up a piece of whisper-pink cloth. She flipped a switch on one of those electrical things that have lots of outlets and the Christmas lights twinkled like stars. Then she turned on the camping lantern. It looked so cozy! We all looked at each other and smiled.

"It looks wonderful, Zuzu," I said. Her eyes closed and her smile took over practically every inch of her face.

"I wish Helen could see it in here," said Bella.

"Yeah," said Zuzu. "I think she'd like it. It looks like a Palace Beautiful."

Calamity curled up in the folds of Bella's skirt.

Bella reached into a big oil-slick-black bag she was carrying and pulled out some matches and a long black candle with a brassy-fake gold candleholder.

"I think we should honor Helen's memory by lighting this candle when we read—sort of like our own private ritual. Let's set it next to the one she left here."

"I think we should have some beautiful art to decorate the walls," said Zuzu. She took my painting and tacked it up with a glittery flower-shaped thumbtack. "That was my favorite thumbtack," she said to me.

I reached over and hugged her. "Thank you."

Bella struck a match and lit the candle. Zuzu took the journal from its sparkly place of honor and said, "I think we should each read like five entries every time. That way, we can enjoy it longer."

"Five's too much," I said. "It will be over too fast. Let's just read one each."

"One?! That would take forever! It has to be five each!"
Zuzu folded her arms hard.

"One!" I insisted, folding my arms as well.

"Five!"

Bella must not have been used to this kind of sister stuff. Her eyes were wide and she looked alarmed. "How about two?" she said. "We just read two each. With the three of us, that's six each time. Besides, some of the entries are pretty short."

Zuzu and I looked at each other. We nodded.

Zuzu handed the journal to me and said, "Two." I began to read.

September 27, 1918

Lizzy and I harvested squash from the garden today. We didn't get as many as we hoped, but there are still quite a few that aren't ripe yet. Mother made them into buttery, spicy pies. Rachel stayed inside to help with the baking. Anna tried to help us pick "quash" as she calls it, but some of them were almost as big as her. She got distracted by a little white butterfly and chased it all over the yard while Lizzy and I worked.

Mother wasn't feeling well today. She never complains, but we all know it is time for the baby to come very soon. She went to bed early—just after supper—and Lizzy and I washed the dishes.

I love my new sewing roll. Today I made Anna's doll Millie a little pillow out of scraps. Anna was so excited, she carried the pillow around all day, and now it's completely covered with dirt from chasing the butterfly and jam from her lunch. I'm going to make a little patch quilt for Rachel's doll Margaret.

After supper, Father read us a chapter from The Pilgrim's Progress. *He read about the Palace Beautiful. He says a man's home is a Palace Beautiful—a place of rest, refuge and beauty where the glory of Heaven is in view. He said that is why he no longer takes the newspaper here: he doesn't want the war invading our home. He said the world can knock all it wants, but unless we open the door, it can't come in.*

I love the idea of our home being a Palace Beautiful! That is exactly what it feels like to me. Lizzy seemed more interested in the frayed hem of her dress than Father's reading. She hates religious texts. She likes novels. Besides, she'd rather work on her sewing. She is a wonderful seamstress. She made the prettiest yellow dress last year that was so fine, she could have sold it in a shop. Anna fell asleep on Rachel's lap. Rachel and I listened to Father's reading. It is my favorite part of the day, no matter what he is reading. Rachel loves it, too. She is always reading when she isn't helping Mother or one of us. I guess she helps more than she reads, but I would guess that if she had all the time in the world, she would spend it in the garden with a book.

It's time to go to bed. I'll write again soon.

—Helen

September 28, 1918

Last night after we went to bed, I heard noises downstairs. I went down to find out what it was. When I got to the bottom of the steps, Father and Doctor Snow were talking. They saw me and told me to go upstairs and to not come down until morning.

I went back upstairs, but I couldn't sleep. I knew Mother was bringing the baby into the world and I couldn't close my eyes.

I tossed and turned so much that Lizzy kicked me and told me to be still. It felt like I lay awake for a hundred years, but finally, I closed my eyes and fell asleep.

When the sun came up, I dashed downstairs. I heard the baby's cry even before I reached Mother and Father's room.

"You girls have a new brother," said Father. "His name is Alfred Walter White."

A brother—I know good and well what a brother means. It means don't get attached.

I stepped into Mother's room. She looked tired and her hair was hanging down across her shoulders. She held a bundle in her arms.

"Come meet little Freddy," she said.

"No, thank you," I said and went back to bed.

Lizzy, Rachel and Anna doted over him all day, but I know he won't last through the night. We were not meant to have a boy grow up in our family. Father says when people die, they are still part of the family, but I don't see little Edward, Joseph or Thomas running around the yard chasing butterflies with Anna or helping us with chores or reading with the family at night, and I don't see Freddy doing it either. I've made up my mind. I won't love my little brother.

—Helen

I handed the book to Zuzu and she took it up reverently and carefully like it was baby Freddy himself. She began to read.

September 29, 1918

Today we went to church. Mother and Freddy stayed home to rest. Bishop Ayers announced the birth and all the women made a fuss. I'm tired of hearing about the baby and talking about the baby. For all the talk about him, you'd think he'd drafted the Constitution or something.

After services Martha Phelps and I took a walk. Martha is my very best friend. I have lots of regular friends, but Martha is my favorite. I'm her favorite, too. That's what makes it nice. We are almost the same age. She was born a week before me and we have made a pact to die a week apart when we are old women. That way things are fair.

Father always stays late at church and discusses the war with the men. Martha's brother Tom is fighting in France and she doesn't like to hear about it. Lots of boys from our town are fighting. Some of them have died. I can't imagine things could get any worse than when people can't keep the war out of their own homes.

We had a nice walk. The weather was fine and warm, but with a hint of autumn in the breeze. Martha and I filled our pockets with crab apples from the trees by the creek. Her brother Paul and his best friend Charlie Moody picked crab apples, too. They threw them at us until we both screamed and ran away. Paul is fifteen and too young to be away fighting like Tom, so he gets to stay home and pester Martha.

When we got back to the church, Anna was crying. She was so worn out from all the excitement of the new baby and all the extra attention, she needed to go home and take a nap. The Phelpses live just across the street from us. They usually walk home with us, but Mrs. Phelps needed to stay late at church, so they didn't this time. We said good-bye to Martha and walked home. I carried Anna all the way.

When we got home, Mother called me into her room. I sat down on the bed and she handed me the baby. She said she had noticed that I had not had a chance to hold him yet. I wanted to say that I didn't want a chance and that it is no use getting attached, but I didn't want to be disrespectful.

Freddy squirmed in his blankets. He has lots of thick dark hair sticking straight up. He bit his tiny fist and grunted. He felt so warm and he smelled so nice that I gave him right back to Mother so I wouldn't be tempted to play with him. I kissed Mother and went to the kitchen to help Lizzy and Rachel with lunch.

Lizzy was disappointed to come home from church early. She usually likes to walk home with her beau Matthew Stoker. I don't have a beau. I don't care to have one either. Martha says she wishes Paul would be my beau so someday we could get married. Then Martha and I would be sisters. But I don't want a beau— especially one who pelts a girl with crab apples. I would only have a beau who was desperately in love with me, and if he was desperately in love with me, he'd never throw crab apples at me.

Father left home before we even sat down at the table. Brother Brown came and asked Father to go with him to administer blessings to a family a few streets over who had been taken ill. He left and we ate dinner without him.

Sundays we rest and read scriptures. With Mother in bed and Father gone, I was tempted to skip reading scriptures and read a novel instead, but I knew better. Besides, Rachel would probably tell.

Anna threw a huge tantrum at bedtime because she wanted her doll Millie to have her hair tied up in braids. We tried to explain that Millie's hair is porcelain and can't be braided, but she just couldn't understand. She kicked and screamed and there was no reasoning with her. Rachel took some brown wool from the knitting basket and made a braided wig. She tied it onto Millie's head with a red ribbon. I thought it looked ridiculous, but it pacified Anna and she finally went to sleep. Rachel always knows what to do.

I will be glad to stop resting and go to school tomorrow.

—Helen

September 30, 1918

At breakfast, Father was tired. He had stayed with the ill family until the early hours.

When breakfast was cleared, he still sat at the table
with his head in his hands. I asked him how the family
was this morning. He said, "Dead." His word felt like a
slap, and I had to sit down in a chair to comprehend it.
He didn't try to comfort me or to smooth things over. He
just sat with his head in his hands and his eyes closed.

We went to school, but I felt a heaviness that made it
hard to concentrate. I kept thinking of the ill family and
Father's tired face.

Tonight, Father seemed to be more himself, but I
could tell he was still thinking about the family. I was still
thinking about them, too.

—Helen

Zuzu handed the book to Bella. Bella took it and sighed.
She looked at the candle in the corner like she was preparing
for a great speech. The light from the candle jumped and
danced around the room. It felt solemn and reverent. Bella
sighed again and began.

October 1, 1918
After school, I went to Martha's house. I brought my
sewing roll and three skirts that needed hemming. I hate
hemming, but I don't mind it if I can visit with Martha
while we do it.

Martha is working on a blouse. It's white with store
lace in two strips straight down the front. It is going to be
so pretty!

I told Martha about the family Brother Brown and
Father tried to help. She said she had heard about several
other families across town that fell ill, too.

I didn't want to talk about it or hear about it anymore.
Fortunately, Martha's mother came in and gave us some
cake and lemonade. She asked how the baby was
doing and Martha said, "Helen does not know, she is not
interested."

I blushed and told Mrs. Phelps the baby is fine.
Martha is always accidentally embarrassing me or herself.
Once, a couple of years ago, we were in class and I was
fidgeting. Martha raised her hand and the teacher asked
what she wanted. She said, "Miss Tanner, may Helen be
excused, I think she needs to use the outhouse." I thought
I was going to die! The rest of the week, all the kids kept
coming up to me and saying, "Do you need me to ask
Teacher if you can go to the outhouse?"

I stayed at the Phelpses' until it was time for chores
and homework, and then I went home.

—Helen

October 2, 1918

Mother is starting to get around more. Sister
Young came over to help with the laundry, but she kept
having to tell Mother to go back to bed. I don't think
Mother likes not being able to do all the things she's used
to doing.

Freddy is a happy baby. He loves Rachel especially.
Rachel has become his other mother. She dresses him,

bathes him and plays with him. I think they are both
thrilled with the arrangement.

I still refuse to hold him, and it is starting to worry
Mother and annoy Lizzy and Rachel. I say, too bad.

This evening, I started thinking about the sick families
again. I wished I could just get away to a place where
people don't get sick, where there is no war and where
baby brothers don't die. I took a spare quilt, my journal
and a candle and went to the attic. I went inside the crawl
space and spread out the blanket. I'm writing from there
right now. I've decided to make this my safe place, my
refuge from the storm, my very own Palace Beautiful. It
is quite comfortable here and I think I'll stay until
bedtime.

—Helen

It seemed to me that the walls of the little crawl space
came alive with old sounds and smells, and it was surprising
that we weren't back in 1918. Calamity stirred and began to
stretch, showing her tiny pin-prick claws and teeth. I imagined what this place had smelled like sixty-seven years ago
when Helen wrote her journal. It probably smelled like fresh
wood and paint. Today, in 1985, it smelled like stagnant dust,
and old. I smelled rain and heard it tapping against the attic
windows. I wondered if Helen ever sat here and heard the
same sound from these same windows.

Bella closed the journal. "That's them!" she said, touching
the black-and-white picture tacked to the wall. We all crowded
around it. Helen's parents were sitting in chairs in the front.

Anna sat on her father's knee and Freddy was on his mother's lap with a fist in his mouth. Lizzy, Rachel and Helen stood behind them.

It was strange, but it felt like I hadn't seen them before when I'd looked at the photo. Now that I knew who they were, it was totally different. I wanted to look at it all day. I wanted to be with them. I wanted to be with my own mother.

Zuzu squinted and touched the photograph. "Father, Mother, Lizzy, Helen, Rachel, Anna and Freddy," she whispered to herself as she passed her finger over each person in the photo. "Freddy looks like a girl!"

"They dressed all babies in gowns back then—even boys," said Bella.

"Well, if Sherrie has a boy, I'll never in a trillion-zillion years let her put a dress on him!"

"When's your mom going to have the baby?" Bella said, leaning back against the wall.

"She's our stepmom. Our real mom's dead," said Zuzu.

"Oh, I'm so sorry! What happened?"

"Childbirth—with Zuzu." I heard something in my own voice that startled me. My throat pinched and I didn't want to look at Zuzu.

It was anger. Sometimes when I thought about my mom dying, I felt mad at Zuzu. Sometimes I felt so mad, I had to hit something. Sometimes the anger bubbled up into a searing-red rage so intense, it scared me. My brain knew it wasn't Zuzu's fault and that I wasn't really mad at her, but another part of me had to blame it on something—anything—and sometimes Zuzu was the easiest target.

"Oh," said Bella, looking at the floor like she felt embarrassed for asking.

"The baby's due in six weeks," said Zuzu.

"Is it a boy or a girl?"

"We don't know. Sherrie doesn't want to spoil the surprise."

"Hmm," said Bella. "I think it would still be surprising to have a whole person come out of your body whether you knew what it was or not, but that's just me."

"I guess it would," I said. Zuzu just blushed and shook her head.

Suddenly Bella's face lit up. "What if we found her?" she said.

"Who?" said Zuzu.

"Helen. If she was born in 1905, she would be eighty years old right now. Maybe she still lives in Utah."

"What if she's dead?" I asked.

"If she is," Bella said softly, "she could be here right now."

We sat silently looking around the little room. My goose bumps came back, and I rubbed my arms to try to stop them.

"Do you think she would haunt us?" Zuzu whispered.

Bella leaned over and blew out the candle. Smoke curled up from the charred wick like spirit fingers. I wasn't sure I actually believed in ghosts, but as we sat watching the thin fingers of smoke wrap around the little space, my skin puckered and pricked.

Bella put her hands on our shoulders and whispered, "But what if she's alive?"

We all looked at each other in silence.

After a minute Zuzu said, "Where do we start? I mean, how does a person find someone who might or might not be dead when they don't know anything about them?"

"We do know some things," I said, picking up the journal. "We know she lived in this house. We know her birthday. We know that if she was thirteen years old in 1918, she would be eighty years old. Lots of people live to be eighty. We know her father had a law practice here in Salt Lake City at one time. We know her full name and even her mother's maiden name."

"Let's do it!" Zuzu said.

Bella looked at the scratched-silver watch on her cave-dwelling-white wrist.

"I have to go!" she said, her honey-black eyes large and round. "I told my mom I'd be home at nine. She said if I was late and if I don't get my chores done, I can't come to the Bonnie Mae party tonight, and it's five after!"

"I'm sure your mom won't mind you being a few minutes late," I said, following her out of Palace Beautiful.

"You don't know my mom." With that, she bounded out of the attic and down the stairs without even saying good-bye.

Zuzu and I laid the journal back in its place of honor and turned out the lights. We left the little room and hid the opening with the wooden crates. A thin trail of leftover smoke from the candle followed us like a spirit out the little doorway and stopped at the stairs.

Nail-Polish Pink

ZUZU AND I SPREAD THE NAIL-POLISH-pink cloth over the card table and everything felt normal again. When a person reaches the age of thirteen, like me, they begin to understand the beauty of sameness. Zuzu and I had probably spread out the tablecloth for Sherrie's Bonnie Mae cosmetic parties a dozen times, and today it made our new house feel even more like our home.

Later, we would greet guests and help seat them. Then the party would begin. Sherrie would have everyone put their name on a little slip of paper and put it in the nail-polish-pink jar. Sherrie would draw a name and, as a demonstration, that person got a free makeover.

When Sherrie was about to be done with the makeover, she would tell everyone the Bonnie Mae threefold key to true beauty. That was Zuzu's and my cue to get the case of free samples. That was everyone's favorite part, and Sherrie let us hand them out. Zuzu and I loved that part, too.

Then, Sherrie would reveal the makeover results and everyone would "ooh" and "aah" and she would tell the made-over woman she looked just like Jackie O. While everyone admired their friend's new look, Zuzu and I would hand out order forms. Then Sherrie, Zuzu and I would busy ourselves so the women would have time to place their orders. Sherrie would tell them that they were the greatest group she had ever worked with and she always meant it. Then everyone would eat.

It was always the same, but because our house and everything else had shifted and moved to the mountains, it felt extra nice to hold the corners of the tablecloth with Zuzu and smooth it just like we had in Houston.

At seven o'clock Grandma Brooks and her friends knocked on the door. The gaggle of old ladies shuffled off to the parlor, and Zuzu and I helped them into the folding chairs.

After a few minutes, more women filed in, including Bella and her mom.

"Holly and Bella!" cried Sherrie, like they were long-lost friends she hadn't seen for decades. "I'm so happy you could make it! Sadie, Zuzu, look who's here!"

"Hi," said Bella shyly. She looked different than she had earlier in the day in Palace Beautiful. She looked like all the color inside her had gone away. If I was going to do a portrait of her at that moment, I would have used empty-nothing white and just-plain black.

"I'm glad you didn't get in trouble for being late earlier," I said.

"I did get in trouble. I have to do all the dishes for the next week by myself, but my mom said I could still come to the party. She said she didn't want the new neighbors to think we were unsocial."

It seemed strange to me that Bella's mom would base a punishment on what the neighbors would think, but that's grown-ups for you. They don't always make much sense.

Holly was wearing an outfit that looked like she was about to play tennis or serve lemonade to people playing tennis. Her skirt was pressed so that there were little straight lines creased on either side. She didn't look a thing like Bella, and I wondered how they could possibly be related. Then I saw it. Holly looked at me and said hello. I saw a little piece of Bella around the corners of her mouth, and she had Bella's honey-black eyes. I had never noticed them before because with a person like Holly, the first thing you notice isn't her eyes or her smile, it's what she's wearing. I wondered why that was.

Even though we'd just moved into town, Sherrie was already making friends and there were a fair amount of people at the party. A lot of them where Grandma Brooks' friends, but a surprising number were people Sherrie had already met in the neighborhood.

Sherrie was one of those people who seemed to know everyone instantly. I remember her talking with the checker at a brand-new grocery store a few years ago. They had been in line maybe five minutes when Sherrie was saying, "Well, Vivian, I hope your mother's hip heals well and that your son can get back on his feet and out on his own. I feel for you, honey!"

When everyone was seated, Sherrie stood up in front of the group and the party went just like it always did in Houston.

Zuzu and I usually hung out in the kitchen or played a game in the back room until it was time for us to help. This time, we decided we wanted to sit by Bella and listen to Sherrie's presentation.

When I sat down next to Bella, I whispered, "Are you okay?"

She reached over and slipped something into my hand. "It's for Palace Beautiful," she whispered so quietly, she was almost not talking at all.

"Shhhh!" hissed her mother, and Bella obediently turned her honey-black eyes to Sherrie. Holly instantly turned back to the presentation and smiled her perfect smile. I didn't like her.

I opened my hand. It was another glass crystal like the one she had given me when we met.

"It's perfect," I said as quietly as I could. Then I whispered, "How many of these ladies do you think are ghosts?"

Bella smiled and some little spark inside her looked like Bella again.

"I was just wondering about that one right there in the lavender top." She nodded in the lady's direction. "I've seen most of these women in the neighborhood, but I don't remember ever seeing her."

"I was wondering about her, too," I said. "You better write it down. Do you have your notebook?"

Bella took my hand and squeezed it. "Let's be friends always," she said.

"We already are."

Holly gave Bella a fierce look and we stopped talking.

"Y'all have been one of the greatest groups I've ever worked with!" said Sherrie. "Okay, before I reveal Mrs. Floyd's makeover result, I want to tell y'all the three most important things you'll hear tonight." Ladies shuffled with their purses, reaching for notebooks and pens. "I'll wait till everyone's ready because if you go away with anything tonight, I want it to be this." The room got silent. "According to Ms. Bonnie Mae herself, the key to true beauty is threefold. One: apply liberally; two: cover completely; and three: blend, blend, blend. I hope everyone got that. Let's say it together. One: apply liberally; two: cover completely; and three: blend, blend, blend."

Zuzu and I took the cue and gave out the free samples. Zuzu was smiling bigger than she had since we left Texas. I knew she felt the comfort of the sameness like I did, even though she was only nine.

"And now for the moment we've all been waiting for," said Sherrie. "Come on out, Mrs. Floyd!"

Mrs. Floyd came out from behind the wall that separated the dining room and the parlor. Everyone oohed and aahed.

"Doesn't she look just like Jackie O!" Sherrie beamed, holding Mrs. Floyd by the shoulders. Mrs. Floyd looked bashfully at the crowd of friends, put her hand to her face and giggled. It looked to me like if she hadn't applied liberally, covered completely and blended, everyone would see her cheeks turning spontaneous-combustion scarlet.

We could usually tell right from the beginning who was going to order and who was just there for the free refreshments. A few women, mostly housewives, usually ordered at least an Everyday Elegance Gift Set. Women with jobs usually ordered the Ms. Mae Career Color Palette. If there were teenage girls in the group, Sherrie could usually talk them into eyeliner or a lipstick from the Totally Mae collection—a line of cosmetics specially formulated for young women. As far as I could tell, "specially formulated for young women" meant that a lipstick costs five dollars instead of twelve.

"I'll put it in Palace Beautiful tonight," I said to Bella over carrot and celery sticks when the official demonstration was over and everyone was visiting and eating hors d'oeuvres.

"What?" asked Zuzu, coming up behind us with her little plastic plate heaped with cookies. I held out the crystal.

"Bella brought it for Palace Beautiful," I said.

"Perfect!" Zuzu said. "Have you thought any more about where to start finding you-know-who?" she whispered, squinting to look mysterious, then stuffing a cookie into her mouth.

"I thought," started Bella. She looked across the room at her mother, who was busy visiting with one of the older ladies. "That is, I think . . ." She looked at her feet.

"What?" said Zuzu, almost dropping her plate.

"I think I already found her."

"Helen?" I said. It felt like the room disappeared and the

only people left were us three. "Where?" I caught myself talking louder than I meant to. Bella's mom looked over, and Zuzu and I both picked up carrot sticks and stuffed them into our mouths, trying to look natural. I'm sure it didn't work, but she ignored us anyway.

"This afternoon, I was in my attic. I looked over and saw a light in yours," said Bella.

"What kind of light?" asked Zuzu.

"It was like a candle, only brighter, and it floated across the room. I watched it for a minute, and then it was just gone."

"Zuzu! What were you doing in the attic?" I said.

"Nothing! I mean I wasn't in the attic! Maybe it was Dad or Sherrie."

"They weren't home, remember!"

We caught ourselves talking loudly again. This time, trying to act natural didn't work. Bella's mom set her plate down and walked over to us.

"Kristin," she whispered sharply. She looked away from Bella and around the room with her big smile that seemed fake, although it was hard to say exactly why. "Time to go now," she said, her teeth tightly together.

"But Mom!" said Bella.

"Kristin!" she snapped, still in a half whisper. "Don't make a scene."

I wondered where Holly had come from. I knew it wasn't the Great Dog or the red birds. It's always hard to tell where a person came from when they are trying to appear a certain way. Looks can be very different from what really is. All I knew was that I didn't like the way she treated Bella. I had known her only a few days, but I knew what I saw.

"Thanks so much, Sherrie," said Holly, picking up her purse while holding Bella by the arm. "Are you sure you don't need help cleaning up?"

"No, thanks, Holly. I think the girls and I can handle it just fine. I'm glad you and Bella could come!"

Holly pulled Bella out the front door.

By ten o'clock, order forms sat in a messy pile on the dining room table, refreshment trays lay picked over and mostly empty on the kitchen counter, and Sherrie, Zuzu and I put everything away for next month.

"It looks like a good night, girls," Sherrie said. "We probably pulled in three hundred dollars. Thanks for all your help." She kissed us on our foreheads.

The evening had gone smoothly and predictably. The only difference was the way Sherrie walked to put everything away—slow and tired—and the way she kept taking breaks to sit down. She would try to sneak them in when she thought Zuzu and I weren't looking.

"Is the baby moving a lot tonight?" I said, catching Sherrie in the act of sitting in the easy chair.

"Come on over here," Sherrie said, so I walked to the chair. She took my hand and placed it on her belly. At first all I felt was the smooth cotton of her breezy-summer-white maternity blouse.

"Just wait for a minute," she whispered. Suddenly, a bump arched across her stomach from left to right. "That's the baby's little back," Sherrie said. "It's turning over." I put both hands on her round bump and felt the baby rolling around inside her.

"Wow!" I said. "What does that feel like?"

"At first, it was like a little goldfish swimming around in there," said Sherrie. "Now . . . well, now it feels like . . . I guess it just feels like a person. An uncomfortable person just trying to get comfortable." She smiled.

"Do you . . . do you ever have dreams about things?" I asked, sitting on the floor beside the easy chair.

"What do you mean?"

"I mean do you have dreams about the baby, me, Zuzu and Dad?"

"Sure."

"What are they like?"

"Usually too silly to mention, like the one I had a few nights ago where we were all watching TV and I realized I'd made a snowman in the living room and forgotten about it and it was melting all over the place."

I giggled. She did, too.

I kissed Sherrie's stomach.

"It's okay to be sad sometimes, Sugar," she said.

"I know. It's okay to be tired sometimes, too."

She looked at me and smiled. "Who's tired?" she said. She lifted herself off the chair and finished cleaning up. She was still radiant. I wondered if Jackie O. could hold up as well as Sherrie on nights like this. Maybe Sherrie was more like Jackie O. than Jackie O. herself.

When everything was put away, we said good night and

dragged our exhausted bodies to bed. After I was sure Dad and Sherrie were down for the night, Zuzu and I hung up the crystal in Palace Beautiful. We were so tired that we didn't even talk, and we each went straight back to our rooms. I fell asleep and dreamed of a light moving slowly across the attic floor.

Thin-Sick Green

I WOKE UP STARTLED AS A HUGE CLAP of thunder shook the house. It was past midnight, but not morning yet. Rain and the sycamore branches beat against the window like they were trying to get in with everything they had. I couldn't get back to sleep.

I reached down to pet Calamity. She purred softly when my fingers touched her fur. Then, I heard something. I sat up. I thought of the light moving across the attic. I heard the floorboards creaking. It sounded like it was coming from downstairs. I remembered what Bella said about Helen and wondered if ghosts can haunt an entire house. Maybe Helen walked not only the attic, but the rest of the house as well.

I listened and heard more sounds. They were definitely footsteps, and they were definitely coming from downstairs. Part of me wanted to go down and see for myself—the part of me that didn't even believe in ghosts. Yet another part of me wanted to run back to Houston and never set foot in this house again.

I put on my slippers and took the flashlight downstairs. The kitchen light was on, and whoever or whatever was stirring in the dark house was there. I crept around the corner and peered in. Sherrie looked up from the kitchen table and jumped almost out of her chair.

"Sadie, sugar, you scared the daylights out of me! What are you doing up?"

I felt too stupid and childish to tell the truth, so I said, "I just needed a glass of milk."

"Well, come on over and have a seat," she said, patting the chair next to her. She was sitting at the table with a glass of water. Sherrie drank lots of water. She says it's the best thing for a youthful complexion. She looked up at me. She didn't look right.

"Are you okay, Sherrie?" I asked, sitting down next to her.

"I don't know," she said. Her answer caught me off guard. Sherrie always said she was fine, or great or terrific—even if we knew good and well she wasn't. A sick feeling of alarm washed over me and I just wanted everything to be normal.

"What's wrong?"

She took my hand and placed it on top of her belly. I didn't feel anything.

"What is it?" Just as I asked that, I felt a bunching up, like a hard knot just under my hand. Sherrie closed her eyes tightly and breathed out in tiny puffs. It looked like she was going into some kind of trance. In a minute it was over and she opened her eyes again.

"What's going on?" I asked.

"Contractions," she said.

"But the baby's not coming for another six weeks."

"That's for the baby to decide. In the meantime, I think I better put my feet up a little." Sherrie sighed. She took a big swallow of her water.

"I can help," I said, feeling a desperate need to make everything okay. "I can take care of Zuzu if you want or fold the laundry."

Just then, Sherrie closed her eyes again, but this time, in between puffs, she said, "Sugar, do you mind getting your dad for me?"

I panicked and ran to the bedroom and shook Dad awake.

"Sherrie!" I yelled.

"What?" Dad asked, in the confusing fog between sleeping and waking.

"Sherrie wants you in the kitchen!"

"What?"

"She's having contractions and she told me to get you."

Dad jumped out of bed like it was spring-loaded and darted into the kitchen. I sat on their bed and put my head in my hands. Thunder rolled all over the house and lightning lit the corners, throwing shadows and flashes of thin-sick-green light in strange unnatural angles across the bedroom. I ran to the kitchen.

"Sadie, I'm going to take Sherrie to the hospital. It's probably nothing, but we just want to be sure. I just called Grandma and she's going to come over and sleep here for the night." Almost instantly, there was a knock at the door. Dad opened it and let in a soaked Grandma Brooks. No one even seemed to notice I was in the room anymore. Grandma and Dad hovered around Sherrie, getting her shoes, a sweater and her hospital bag, which had been packed since we were in Houston.

I watched as they helped her into the car and then ran up to my room. I couldn't sleep. I thought about Sherrie at the hospital and wondered what they were doing to her. I thought about my mom. I wondered what look was on her face when she died. Was she afraid? I wondered what the house would feel like if Dad came home without Sherrie.

The storm blew outside and I was afraid the sycamore would break through my window. What if the outside came in? What if all the good and warm things blew away and I couldn't stop it? What if my room felt safe and I still lost Sherrie? What if there really was no safe place?

Cozy-Sugar Brown

THE NEXT MORNING THE STORM WAS over and Sherrie and Dad came home from the hospital.

"False alarm," said Sherrie, smiling at me from the breakfast table. She was in her bathrobe and coochy-coo-pink fuzzy slippers. The radio was playing the news. President Reagan was talking about some crisis somewhere in the world, and I didn't want to hear any more bad news. I turned it off and sat at the table with a bowl of cereal.

"Not entirely," said Dad. "The doctor said the baby could come early if Sherrie doesn't take it easy. I'll need you and Zuzu to help out around the house."

"Oh, Norman!" Sherrie threw up her hands. "Sadie helps out plenty!" She turned to me. "Sugar, you just enjoy yourself and get to know the neighborhood. We'll manage just fine."

"Sherrie," Dad said, like he was talking to a little kid.

"Norman," she replied in a mocking tone. Then she

squinted, puffed out her breath, and put her hand on top of her stomach like she had the night before.

"Why don't you go lie down," said Dad. "Sadie and I will bring breakfast to you."

She didn't argue and went off to bed.

"Where's Grandma?" I asked.

"She's in the garden. She's going to stay with you girls and Sherrie today while I go to a meeting at the university."

At that moment, Zuzu came stomping down the stairs still half asleep. She marched into the kitchen.

"Hey! Who ate all the Frosty Cocoa Flakes?" she shouted. "Now all that's left is Crunchy Oat Bran Fiber Nuggets! This family is so unfair!"

Zuzu had slept through everything. She didn't know anything was different.

"Zuzu, be quiet! Sherrie's not feeling well," I said.

"What's wrong with her?" she asked, setting her bowl on the table.

"The doctor says the baby could come too early if she doesn't take it easy," Dad explained.

I noticed Dad's face for the first time that morning. His brow wrinkled with worry and his cheeks sagged. He looked like he'd been beaten up. He looked old.

"You okay, Dad?" I said.

"What? Oh, yeah," he answered, patting me on the head absently like I was a puppy. "Yeah, I'm fine—just a little tired, that's all."

I watched his body move slowly into his chair. His shoulders looked tense and tight, but the rest of his body looked

Cozy-Sugar Brown

limp and defeated. For the first time, I saw him as a man—not just Dad. For the first time, I saw him as someone who had lost the one he loved and was afraid of losing again.

"I can do the dishes," I said.

Dad looked up at me and smiled. "That would be nice."

I looked at Zuzu obliviously eating her cereal and felt the anger and fear welling up inside me. I was able to push it back down before it spilled over. I wondered if it would ever go away entirely. It had been inside me so long, it was just part of my body.

Just then, the doorbell rang.

"It's Bella," I said. "Dad, is it okay if she comes over? We won't be any trouble at all, I promise."

"If it's okay with Grandma," said Dad.

I looked out the kitchen window and saw Grandma in the garden pruning a scraggly hedge and singing to herself. I knew it would be okay. That is one thing I love about Grandma Brooks. Zuzu put down her cereal spoon and ran outside to ask, but we already knew the answer.

I opened the door and Bella walked in like it was her own house.

"I brought my notebook," she whispered. "Have you seen the light in the attic yet?"

"No, we were waiting for you," I said.

Bella beamed and looked at her feet bashfully.

Zuzu and Bella gathered up the dishes and put them in the new dishwasher.

I poured cat food into a little nail-polish-pink bowl that used to be part of the Bonnie Mae display. I poured water into a little Blue Willow dish that Grandma Brooks gave Sherrie for Christmas. Sherrie had said it was okay. Besides, Bonnie Mae and Blue Willow are both a part of my history, and I wanted Calamity to have a piece of it even if she was only a cat. I went upstairs and got her. She was asleep on her pink towels. She mewed and stretched her little paws. I rubbed her feather-soft fur against my cheek and wondered what it felt like for a mother cat to have all those babies rolling around inside her. I was glad for Sherrie that her baby didn't have claws. I took Calamity downstairs and set her by the cat food bowl.

I said good-bye to Dad as he picked up his briefcase and got ready to go to his meeting. Zuzu had run back out to the garden to tell Grandma we would be upstairs. It was the truth; we were going upstairs. She just didn't say how far up.

"Where did you see the ghost?" asked Zuzu once the attic door was safely shut.

"Right there." Bella pointed to the wall opposite Palace Beautiful. "I read that ninety percent of ghosts like to hang around the secret places they had in life. It would make sense that Helen would hang out here. When I'm a ghost, I'm going to haunt the crawl space under my stairs—most likely. I haven't decided for sure."

"What exactly did it look like?" asked Zuzu, scratching her chin, like she was trying to be a private investigator or something.

"It looked like—"

But just before she could get the words out, Dad's car

pulled out of the driveway and the reflection from the windshield cast a bright light on the wall. It moved across the attic as he drove down the street.

"That," she said, dropping her arms at her sides and making her black skirt puff out for a second and then deflate.

"Oh," I said. "Well, we can keep watching and see if we see any more lights or things like that."

Bella didn't say anything. She crawled into Palace Beautiful and we followed. I lit the candle and placed it in the corner and picked up the journal. I read first.

October 3, 1918

Today Lizzy, Martha and I took the trolley into town and bought new Sunday hats. Lizzy ran into Matthew Stoker on the trolley home and I saw them hold hands when they thought no one was looking. Martha hoped to run across Charlie Moody. She has had her eye on him for ages. I can't see why. Paul and Charlie have been best friends since they were babies, and they spend a great deal of time pestering and torturing her. For some reason, she likes Charlie anyway. Well, she saw him at the soda fountain, but as usual, she was too shy to talk to him. Martha's timidity around Charlie annoys Lizzy to no end. She says if Martha is ever to have a chance with him, she has to assert herself. Martha says it is not ladylike, but I think that is just an excuse.

Lizzy and Martha both got the most adorable little blue hats. Mine is gray.

Rachel stayed home and tended Anna and Freddy. We

brought her home a pair of gloves and a peppermint stick. We brought Anna a red ribbon and a peppermint stick.

Mother was up and around more today. She made a big pot of apple butter. The house smells wonderful!

Freddy was fretful today. Mother asked if I would hold him while she and Rachel peeled apples. I did, but I gave him back as soon as I could.

Tonight Father read us more Pilgrim's Progress, and now everyone is in bed—except me, of course. I'm in my own Palace Beautiful. I love my new little place. I took some flowers that I dried and hung them up by the entrance to the crawl space. I think it looks lovely. No one else knows I've taken this space, not even Martha. I want to keep it a secret so that I can always come here to get away and to be by myself.

—Helen

October 4, 1918

Today Lizzy and I picked more apples while Rachel tended Anna and Freddy. Lizzy was in a bad mood and kept telling me I was picking the apples wrong. How in the world can someone pick an apple wrong? She stayed in a bad mood until Matthew Stoker came over and asked to take her on a walk. She came back sweet and smiling. It was like she left as one girl and came back as another.

When Freddy went down for his nap, Rachel took a book and curled up in the grapevine bower and read. At dinnertime, I found her there asleep. I woke her up. Her cheeks were red with too much sunshine and she looked so tired. I think she is worn out from tending Freddy and Anna so much. I offered to take over for a while even though it meant I'd have to actually hold the baby. It seemed only fair. Luckily, Freddy slept most of the afternoon, so I only had to get him ready for bed and carry him around for a while. He fell asleep for the night a few minutes ago.

Father came home from work early. He looked troubled. After we ate, he told us one of his clerks had contracted influenza. He said it was influenza that took that family Sunday. He said it seemed to be spreading across the city. We must have looked worried, because Father reassured us that it will surely run its course like everything else. He said he guessed it will be gone in a week or two. He smiled, but he was sober behind it.

Later, I heard him tell Mother that if the sickness continues for more than a week or two, he'll close his practice until it is gone.

I am scared. Lizzy says I'm being a baby and that sickness is just part of life. I know she is right, but something in my soul feels uneasy.

—Helen

I handed the book to Zuzu. A thin whisper of smoke from the candle wrapped its fingers around the room. It felt like a different place—like we could walk out and it would really be

1918. Zuzu took the book and brushed the curls out of her eyes and began to read.

October 5, 1918

    Today, the sisters from church got together and made gauze masks to combat the spread of influenza. Mother could not attend, but Mrs. Phelps brought over a mask for each of us that she made herself. She even made a tiny one for Freddy. I hate looking at that little mask. I hate influenza. I want things to be normal.

    Mrs. Phelps used to be a nurse before she was married, so she knows all about staying healthy. She has made it her job to see that everyone she knows stays that way. She brought over the Health Department's list of rules to combat the flu. The list says to avoid crowds, breathe through your nose not your mouth, eat healthful foods and chew thoroughly, open windows at night, do not use napkins, spoons, forks, cups, etc. that someone else has used and not washed, avoid tight clothes and breathe deeply. Mrs. Phelps said that she has Martha breathe deeply through her nose ten times every hour and that she won't let her wear her corset until the sickness is gone from the state. I wish my mother made me take off my corset.

    At dinner tonight I tried to chew my food more thoroughly. Lizzy said I was being annoying and to just eat regular. I told her I'd rather be healthy than eat regular. Lizzy rolled her eyes and sighed. Mother told both of us to behave and just eat. I did, but I still chewed thoroughly.

    —Helen

October 6, 1918

Today at church, Bishop Ayres said that several of our ward members are ill with influenza and that city leaders are thinking about closing churches and schools until the outbreak goes away. I heard that it isn't just in Salt Lake City, it's all over the state and all over the country.

The bishop encouraged us to keep worshipping even if we cannot meet together. He encouraged us to pray for the sick of our ward family. I said a silent prayer—but not for the sick. It was for me. I hate all the talk about influenza. Whenever anyone mentions it, I feel a lump in my throat and a sick rush in my stomach. The Health Department gives out little white quarantine cards to put in the front windows of sick houses. There were three on my way to town yesterday. I did not want the bishop to talk about it anymore. I just wanted to go home where we are safe. I wanted to work on my red shawl and play with Anna. I wanted to help Mother with dinner and read with Father. I wanted to curl up in my Palace Beautiful with everything normal and fine.

After church, Martha and I visited in the church garden with some of the other kids from our Sunday school class. Martha kept telling them how her mother had taken away her corsets. I couldn't believe she was saying it in front of everyone! And it wasn't just girls she was telling, there were boys present, too! I kept trying to change the subject, but she kept going back to it. Finally, it was time to walk home. I heard the other kids giggling behind our backs as we left. My face

was bright red and Martha said I must have gotten
sunburned.

This afternoon, some of the men went out and
administered priesthood blessings to the sick. Father was
not asked because he has a new baby at home and
influenza is so contagious. For once, I was glad we had
Freddy. He saved Father from going to the houses with
the white cards in the windows.
—Helen

Zuzu held out the book to Bella. Bella smoothed her skirts
and cleared her throat and took the book from Zuzu. She
read:

October 7, 1918
Right after school we got a family photograph taken.
Freddy and Anna screamed when the flash exploded.
Lizzy laughed and got in trouble for it. I can't wait to see
the print! I hope I have my eyes open. Martha got her
picture taken once, and her mouth was open and her eyes
were closed. It looked so funny, but her parents hung it up
in their parlor anyway. Martha was mortified.

When we got home, I decided to fix up my Palace
Beautiful. I took up a scrub bucket and rag and wiped
down all the walls and the floor. I rubbed so hard, they
almost shine. The little room looks so cozy now!

I can feel the chill of autumn. Palace Beautiful is
quite cold, but I suppose I can bring in more blankets
when winter comes. The house smells like apples again

because Mother baked six pies this afternoon. She is starting to get up more and more. I'm glad. Rachel is tired from tending Freddy—although she'll never say so. Lizzy and I are tired from all the extra cooking, cleaning and mending. Anna is starved for Mother's attention. Even Father is smiling more since Mother has been up. It feels good to have things get back to normal.

I was putting the bucket away when Anna came into the kitchen. She was crying. Her nose and ears were red from playing in the cold backyard. I asked her what the matter was and she held out her hand. Stretched across her palm lay a dead butterfly. I took Anna in my arms and hugged her. Her little shoulders shook up and down and I nearly cried myself.

I told her that her butterfly's spirit is in Heaven now with its family. I told her that we each have a spirit and a body and that our bodies die, but our spirits don't. I tried to tell her that her butterfly is happy and safe and can never die again. She seemed to take comfort and went off to her room to play. I took the butterfly and buried it under the roses in the backyard. I used a spoon to dig the little grave. When it was done, the spoon was such a mess that I buried it next to the butterfly so Lizzy wouldn't get mad at me for ruining Mother's silverware. I don't think anyone will notice. Later, I showed Anna the little grave and she seemed satisfied and started chasing another butterfly.

Rachel and I delivered a pie to the Phelpses and Lizzy took one to the Browns. After dinner, the three of us delivered pies to the Hammonds, the Smiths, and the Riries.

I started crocheting a shawl today. I found the loveliest red wool downtown, and I decided to use the shell pattern Mother used for her own shawl last year. I like crocheting. It's faster than knitting and I can do more creative stitching. Mother told me once that I made the best lace of any girl my age she had ever known. I tried not to take the compliment to heart and get vain, but I'm afraid I remember it every time I pick up a crochet hook. I hope the shawl turns out nicely. I think it will.

Good night.

—Helen

October 8, 1918

Today it rained off and on. The snow levels crept down the mountains and made them look like enormous frosted cakes. The air smells so good! I love autumn! Lizzy, Rachel and I were soaked when we arrived at school, but we didn't mind since everyone else was, too.

We were well into our lessons when I realized Bonnie Lane was not in class. At recess, I heard some of the kids talking about her. They said her family has influenza. I felt the sickness in my stomach and the lump in my throat. I felt like I had to swallow hard. Some of the kids joked about it. They sang,

> I had a little bird
> Whose name was Enza

Cozy-Sugar Brown

> *I opened the window*
> *And influenza.*

I didn't think it was funny at all! I picked up a crab apple and hit one of the kids on the back of the head. He came running after me, but I made it to the schoolhouse before he caught me.

I asked Miss Burbage why Bonnie was not in school today. She told me to ask my mother. I asked her if Bonnie had influenza. Again she told me to ask my mother.

When I got home, I did ask Mother. She told me Bonnie had had influenza and that she was dead. I ran up to my room and cried. I cried harder than I have ever cried in my life. I cried half for Bonnie and half for the terrible feeling in my soul. I want the sickness to go away! I want things to be like they were! I want to feel safe again!

—Helen

I pinched out the candle with my fingertips and smoke swirled around the little room.

"She's going to die," said Zuzu. "I know it. The journal is only half filled. She's going to die and now she haunts our attic!"

"We don't know that, Zuzu," I said. "For all we know, she was just fine and she lives in Fresno or something."

"Fresno?" said Bella.

"I don't know. That was the first thing that came to my mind. We need to think of a place to start looking for her."

"How about the cemetery?" said Bella.

"I know! It's so obvious! Grandma!" I said. "She's lived here forever. She'd know!"

"Yeah! Grandma Brooks!" said Zuzu, almost dashing out the door.

"Wait! She can't know what we are doing." I grabbed Zuzu by the skirt. "We have to ask her in a way that she won't get suspicious. This is our place and it has been a secret all these years and we need to keep it that way."

"Let's go ask Iona, then," Bella said. It felt weird to hear Grandma Brooks called Iona by a kid. It felt even weirder that Bella had probably seen more of Grandma in her life than Zuzu and I had, since they lived on the same street.

"Let's go ask her right now! She's in the garden!" said Zuzu.

We closed up Palace Beautiful and went out to the backyard.

"Good morning, ladies," said Grandma Brooks, wiping her forehead with her sleeve. It was hot and the sun was extra bright. I squinted and my eyes burned until they got used to the light.

"Hi, Iona," said Bella.

"Hello there, Kristin." Grandma set down her pruning shears. "You can call me Grandma Brooks if you like."

"I can call you Grandma Brooks?" Bella said, her honey-black eyes lighting up. "You can call me Belladonna Desolation—or Bella for short if you like."

"All right. How are your sisters?"

"Fine. Linda and her husband live in Detroit and have two kids. Amy got married last year and lives in Atlanta."

"Could they really be that grown up? Things certainly do change fast. How's your mother, Bella? Last night at the party she said she is still doing paperwork for Dr. Silverman?"

"Yeah, she likes it."

"I'm glad to hear that. I was digging in the old garden plot this morning and look what I found." Grandma Brooks reached into her pocket and pulled out what looked like a piece of flat dirt. "I need to clean it off a little, but look, it's a spoon."

She handed it to me. Bella and Zuzu crowded around me to have a look.

"It was silver at one point. It looks pretty old—maybe even older than me." She laughed. We didn't.

"The spoon!" said Zuzu. "The one with the butterfly!"

"What?" asked Grandma.

"Nothing," I said. I glared at Zuzu.

"It looks like it had been there a long time," said Grandma. "These old houses are full of little surprises. Would you girls like a piece of chocolate cake? I brought one from my house."

"Yes!" exclaimed Bella so eagerly she sounded almost like Zuzu. "I mean, I would, thank you."

"And you, Sadie, Zuzu?"

"That would be great," I said.

"Yes, please," said Zuzu, putting on her best manners, but jumping up and down at the same time.

"Well, let's go in and I'll get washed up. You girls can keep the spoon. It belongs to the house."

Bella, Zuzu and I nodded at each other, silently agreeing to put it in Palace Beautiful.

We followed Grandma Brooks into the kitchen. Her house

always smelled like homemade cake and old things, and when she came to our house, she brought the smells with her. I've always loved that old-things smell—the smell of a million stories tucked away in forgotten corners.

She set a pan of cozy-sugar-brown cake on the kitchen table.

"Do you still have your crochet group, Grandma?" asked Zuzu, reaching for the biggest piece of cake.

Grandma Brooks almost always had a crochet hook in her hand. She made afghans, cozies to hide appliances, delicate doilies, bedspreads and wall hangings. Nearly every piece of furniture in her house had some sort of crocheted item covering it, decorating it or just plain lying on it. She had a group of friends that got together every week and crocheted. I remember when my mom died they each crocheted a stuffed animal for Zuzu and me. We got a seal, a puppy, a giraffe, a horse, a bunny, a chicken and a cat. The women had known each other since elementary school and stayed friends for decades and decades. Grandma Brooks always talked about them like they were an extended part of our family.

"Well, I'm sorry to say, over the years our group dwindled down to Nettie and myself, and three months ago Nettie moved to Arizona to be near her daughter."

"I'm so sorry," I said. I remembered how nice they all were.

"Yes, we had a good time together. That is the tough part of getting old—the getting left behind."

"Sometimes you don't have to be old to get left behind," I said almost under my breath.

"That's true, dear," she said, setting a piece of cake in front of me.

Grandma Brooks moved and spoke slowly—not because she was old, but because she was from Adam and Eve and she had become wise. I've always noticed that when people are wise, they seem to do things more slowly—like every movement, every word, every breath makes a difference in the vast universe.

"Grandma Brooks," Zuzu tried to say with her mouth full of cake.

"Zuzu! Don't talk with your mouth full," I said.

"I'm not!" Bits of chocolate cake fell out of her mouth onto the table. She swallowed and continued. "Grandma, we have a few questions for you."

I kicked Zuzu under the table. "Remember it's a secret," I whispered.

"Don't talk with your mouth full, Sadie, it's rude!" She stuck her tongue out at me.

"What do you want to know?" asked Grandma Brooks.

I took over before Zuzu could confess everything. "Do you know who lived in this house before we did?"

"Sure. Bill and Cathy Goodson. They lived here a long time."

"Oh," I said, a little disappointed.

"Do you remember who lived here before them?" asked Bella.

"Let's see. I remember the Kochans way, way back. They had a son who used to play ball with your dad."

"What about when you were a little girl?" I asked, trying not to sound too eager or obvious.

"I suppose the first family I can remember in this house would be the Whites. I was pretty little then, and I don't really remember much. They moved away before I was in school. I think the parents or some of the kids died or something like that and the rest of them moved to be with family, but I'm not sure."

"Influenza," whispered Zuzu. Bella looked at Zuzu and me with her huge eyes like she had seen a ghost.

"Do you remember any of the White kids' names?" asked Zuzu.

"Can't say that I do. It was a long time ago. Why do you ask?"

"Just curious," I said.

"Any more questions?"

"We'll get back to you," said Zuzu, rubbing her chin.

"I have to go home for chores," said Bella. "Could you . . . could you teach me how to crochet?" she asked. "Not today, I know, but maybe . . . maybe tomorrow?"

Grandma's eyes brightened. "I'd love to! What about you girls?" she said, turning to me and Zuzu.

"Uh, okay," I said. Grandma Brooks and Bella both looked so happy, I felt I had to say yes. Zuzu didn't say anything. I looked at her and she rolled her eyes.

"All right," she whined.

"Okay, come back tomorrow and we'll get started."

India Red

"YOU'RE 'IT'!" SHOUTED ZUZU, WAVING her arms and jumping up and down. Her pretty curls bounced up and down after her and flashed in the sunshine.

"No fair! I got you!" yelled a boy I didn't recognize. A swarm of kids who looked about Zuzu's age ran frantically from one end of the yard to the other, shrieking and laughing.

Zuzu had Sherrie's touch for making instant friends. Grandma Brooks had sent her out to play when Bella left, and already Zuzu had a tribe of kids playing in our front yard.

Grandma was lying down on the living room sofa for a quick rest, and I was in charge of taking care of Sherrie without letting Sherrie know we were taking care of her. She didn't like being waited on.

"How are you feeling, Sherrie?" I asked, setting an enormous plastic mug of ice water on her bedside table. I could hear Zuzu's clan shouting and laughing through the window.

"Thanks, Sugar. I'm fine," she said, taking a big swig. "I needed that. Those hospital lights can sure make a woman notice all the little fine lines she didn't know she had."

"How are you really feeling?" I sat down on her bed.

Sherrie inhaled deeply and leaned back on her pillow. "Truthfully?"

"Yes, truthfully."

"Just between us girls?"

"Just between us girls."

Sherrie sighed again and said, "Not so good."

I felt the panic return. I tried to hide it so she would know I was old enough to handle the truth.

"What hurts?"

"It isn't what hurts that feels bad."

"What do you mean?"

"I mean I'm scared."

My stomach gave a jolt and I felt scared, too.

"Oh, Sugar, everything's going to be fine," Sherrie said, putting her hand on mine. "I'll tell you what it feels like," she said. "It feels like I'm at the end of a diving board looking down—way down. It looks farther down than anything I've ever seen before. I know people jump off the diving board every day and are just fine, and I know I'm going to be just fine, but standing there with my toes hanging off the edge is a little scary. Understand?"

"I guess."

"How are you feeling? Truthfully," Sherrie asked.

"I don't know. It's just that everything's changed now and it's going to get even more changed."

"Yes, some things are, but not everything. Your daddy, Zuzu and I still love you. You still have your family—it's just in a new place. Your family's going to get bigger soon, but it's still your same family. The only difference is, when the baby comes, we will be complete. Everyone will be together."

"Not everyone. Not my mom."

Sherrie sat up and put her arm around me. "You're right, Sugar, not your mom. No one can replace your mom. When a person dies, they take their whole universe with them. Each universe is one of a kind, just like that Paris Diva handbag over there in the corner—there isn't another one like it in the world and there never will be. When a universe is gone, it can never be replaced, but there will always be something or someone to pick up where things left off. I can't replace your mom, but I can love you like my own daughter, and I do. I can't love you in the way your mom did because I'm not her, but I can love you in my own way. It may be different, but it's still love. I may not be your actual mother, but we can be the very best of girlfriends."

"Thank you, Sherrie," I said. I tried not to cry. I tried to stuff my tears into a hard lump and swallow them, but one escaped.

"You are just as important to my life as this baby is. There's no difference as far as I'm concerned. I want you to know that."

"I know. Thanks."

"Sugar, could you hand me that green bag on the dresser?"

"Sure." I brought it over to her. Sherrie unzipped it and

pulled out a foggy-morning-gray eyeliner pencil and put it in my hand.

"I found this in my sample bag and thought it would look great on Bella. It's her season. She has the most brilliant eyes, and I think this would really make them pop. Tell her to make sure to blend or it will look like she's trying out for the football team."

I looked at Sherrie and started laughing. She did, too. "Go on now, and have some fun."

I didn't feel like having fun.

I went up to my room and reached under my bed. I pulled out my most prized possession—a box containing things that had belonged to my mother. I tried to look at it every day, but sometimes I forgot, and that was what scared me the most. What if I couldn't remember her India-red watch or her high school photo or the button from her far-far-away-blue jacket? Someone has to remember or it disappears. Someone has to remember each of these little treasures every single day.

Dark-Planet Purple

MY MOM SAID YOU CAN SLEEP OVER IF you want," said Bella, standing in the doorway later that evening.

"Really?" I said, looking past her to the group of kids playing in our yard that was now even larger. Zuzu sat in the center like a queen.

"Yeah, she said you can if you want. I mean if it's okay with your parents."

"Thanks! I'll go ask," I said.

After I packed my backpack, we walked through the crowd of kids to Bella's house.

Her house was big and white. It wasn't brick like ours. It had wooden shingles all over it. The windows all had black shutters, and the front door was black, too. Perfectly shaped bushes wrapped around the house and looked like a shelf. The path to the front door was lined with marigolds and pansies.

"Come on in," said Bella. As soon as we stepped across the threshold, Bella seemed to transform to another girl. She looked pale—paler than usual, like a candle that had been snuffed. She looked like she did the afternoon we met. I didn't realize how much Bella had brightened until I saw her pale and sad in her front doorway.

Bella's house was perfect and immaculate. The furniture was so clean, it looked like no one ever used it. Everything looked modern and straight out of a decorating magazine. It felt like a museum display of a house—all the correct things, but kind of empty with no soul or feeling behind it. I didn't like it. I was almost sorry I had agreed to stay over.

A chandelier hung in the entryway. It dripped with crystals, and I noticed two of the tear-shaped crystals were missing.

Bella took me to her room. The walls were bridesmaid-mauve and the curtains on her tiny window were grandma's-talcum-powder blue. The colors looked nothing like Bella at all. Posters covered nearly every inch of one of her walls. I glanced at the wall, trying to take in each picture.

"Mom says I can hang things only on this wall," she said.

"How come?" I asked.

"She doesn't want me to ruin the paint. That's my favorite band, the Black Morrisons," she said, pointing to a poster with four guys who looked like they were crying charcoal tears. They each had a black long-stem rose clenched in their teeth. The background of the poster was electric-squint pink and dark-planet purple. About half the posters were of the

Black Morrisons. The other half were of horses, advertisements torn out of magazines, and art prints like a person can order from a museum catalog.

"I like this picture," I said, pointing to a tiny clipped magazine photo of an island with a lighthouse on it. Next to the lighthouse was a big apple tree in bloom.

"Huh. Me, too," Bella said without looking to see which picture I was talking about.

I glanced around the room. Bella's bed lay under the little window. A dark dresser and bedside table sat in opposite corners of the room. All of Bella's things had some strange quality that made a person want to look closer—knickknacks that drew in the eye, little bits of this and that. I leaned in to see more. A lot of the stuff looked handmade. I still wasn't certain until I saw her room, but it seemed more likely than ever that she was from the Great Dog and was an artist, too. I thought about the Great Dog as I stood in the room. I could almost hear him throwing back his head and howling in despair.

Something didn't fit, though. She seemed artistic like she was from the Great Dog but, at the same time, shy like she was from Adam and Eve. I knew she wasn't from the cabbage patch, but she didn't seem to fit exactly anywhere. She was just Bella—but what exactly was that?

She took my backpack and placed it on the floor next to a pile of perfect blankets that formed a makeshift bed. "There, all set," she said. She flopped down on her bed and pulled out her zebra notebook.

"So, have you found any new clues . . . ," Bella started to say, when someone knocked on the bedroom door.

"Come in," she called, quickly stuffing the notebook under her pillow.

"Cupcakes," said her mom, opening the door. She was wearing the same apron as the other day and held out a silver tray stacked with pink and white cupcakes, each one sparkling with sugar sprinkles. Holly looked so out of place in Bella's room, it almost seemed funny.

"Thanks, Mom!" said Bella. "My mom makes great cupcakes."

"You girls have a good time." She set the tray on the dresser top and left the room.

"That was nice of her," I said, taking a perfect cupcake from the perfect silver tray.

"She likes to do that kind of thing when we have company."

"I'm not company. I'm just regular old Sadie Evelyn Brooks."

"She never does stuff like this when no one is going to see it but me," Bella said, with her mouth full of cupcake. "I guess it's too much trouble. She's really busy. Sometimes I think . . . sometimes I think I'm extra."

"What do you mean?" I asked, peeling the paper off the pretty pink cupcake.

"I mean, she was tired after she raised my sisters, and then I came along. She was busy doing other things and she still is. Maybe some people aren't supposed to be born. Maybe some people are just extra."

My throat tightened and I felt the rage in my stomach begin to boil. "No one is extra, Bella—especially you!"

"Maybe I am." She didn't look at me when she said it. I could tell that part of her really believed it and that it hurt her like nothing else could hurt.

"Listen, everyone who is here is meant to be here. There are no extras."

"I don't know," said Bella, lying down on her bed, looking at the ceiling. I lay on the makeshift bed, trying hard not to hate Holly.

"My mom goes to bed really early."

"Sherrie, too. She has to get her beauty sleep."

"I don't know if my mom calls it beauty sleep. I think she just gets tired. She does a lot of work at Dr. Silverman's office and at church and the neighborhood community council and all that. She's gone a lot, and when she's home, she's pretty worn out. I clean the house while she's gone so she doesn't have to worry about things when she gets home."

"What kind of cleaning stuff do you do?"

"You know, dust, vacuum, dishes, laundry and all that stuff. I do most of my own cooking, too, except when we have company. I make really good spaghetti."

"At our house, we all do the work, not just one person."

"Oh," said Bella. "Well, my mom is really tired."

"You sound like Cinderella or something," I said. I couldn't look at her because I knew it would only make me more angry at her mother. "Do you go out with friends and stuff?"

"Mom has a rule that she doesn't drive me places. She says it would spoil me and she needs to take care of herself by not driving kids all over the place."

"She doesn't take you anywhere?"

"I can go anywhere, I just have to get a ride from someone else." Bella was quiet for a few minutes. Then she said, "She says I'm difficult. I suppose I am, but part of me feels like it isn't true. I don't know what she wants from me, but I know it's something different from what I am. I try to be it and I just can't. If that's being difficult, then I guess she's right." Bella rolled over onto her stomach. "You know she used to make me go to a shrink after school."

"What for?"

"I don't know. It felt like she was trying to make me into the girl she thought I should be or something." She laughed, but I couldn't see why. I wouldn't laugh if Sherrie did that to me, but she never would. Sherrie liked me no matter what I was like.

"Bella," I started.

"I don't really want to talk about it anymore. Want to listen to the Black Morrisons?"

"Sure," I said.

Bella put a tape in her stereo and we listened.

"After my mom goes to bed, I think we should look for more clues," Bella said.

"What do you mean?"

"I mean, I think we should go to the cemetery." Bella took the notebook back out and waved it.

"Isn't it closed after dark?"

"Yes."

"What about your dad? Won't he be up?"

"He's gone."

Until that moment, I hadn't realized I had never heard Bella refer to her dad. It hadn't crossed my mind that he might not live with them.

"Gone where?"

"He lives in Detroit near my sister. My parents divorced when I was three. I see my dad a few times a year." She flipped through her notebook as she spoke, like she was waving off a pesky fly—no big deal.

"Wow!" I said. I couldn't imagine a week without my dad, let alone him living across the country.

"It's not so bad. I'm used to it."

Bella was right, her mom did go to bed early. The sky wasn't all the way dark yet. The sun had set, but its light was still hanging on in the front yards of our street. Bella and I sat on the porch digging our bare feet into the perfect grass. It felt funny to look over my shoulder and see my own bedroom window, but feel miles away from home.

Zuzu and her friends had disbanded for the night and only older kids were out now. A couple of boys were tossing around a basketball in a driveway across the street and a few doors down.

"That one is Derrick Matthews," said Bella, stretching out her arm and pointing lazily to the boys. "That one, there, is Jason Prince."

As soon as Bella said his name, her cheeks turned fire-alarm red.

"Jason Prince?" I said.

"Yeah," she sighed. "Do you dare me to say hi?"

"What?" I said.

"Do you dare me to go over and say hi?" she repeated, her eyes following Jason like they were electromagnetically attached to him. I couldn't see anything daring at all in saying hi, but she seemed pretty intent.

"Sure," I said.

Bella took me by the hand and jumped off the porch. She dashed across the street, dragging me behind her. She stopped at the end of the driveway where the boys were playing.

"Hi, Bella," said Jason, picking up the basketball and holding it against his hip. He *was* good-looking, and I could see why Bella blushed. He was tall with olive skin and matching honey-black hair and eyes like Bella's. I couldn't help noticing Derrick, too. He was tall and solid with in-between brown hair—like it was probably baby-chick blond when he was little and was going to be dark when he was grown. He smiled at me and I almost blushed.

Bella stood frozen and silent. I waited for her to say something—anything. When it didn't happen, I said, "I'm Sadie. I just moved in over there." I pointed to my house.

"Nice to meet you, Sadie. I'm Jason and this is Derrick," he said, nodding toward the other boy.

"It's nice to meet you," I said. Bella still stood staring and frozen. I poked her with my elbow.

"Hi, Jason!" she said, almost shouting the words just to get them out. Then she grabbed me by the hand again and ran back across the street and into her house, slowing down only to close the door quietly. We ran into her room. She flopped down on her bed and let out a huge sigh.

"Did you hear the way he said, 'Hi, Bella'?" she said, gazing not so much at the ceiling as right through it.

"Yeah," I said.

"And how I came across the street and said hi to him for no real reason?"

"Yeah."

"I wonder if he thought I was bold and mysterious."

"Sure. He probably did," I said, lying down on the makeshift blanket bed.

"Yeah," Bella said, smiling so big, she almost glowed. "Yeah."

Clenched-Fist Gray

NIGHT IN SALT LAKE CITY IS THE BEST time of all. All the heat mellows and the mountains breathe out clean, cool air. Bella and I each took a flashlight from her laundry room, and the zebra-striped notebook, and headed for the cemetery.

Bella's mom was sound asleep. Before we left, we opened her bedroom door just a tiny crack and heard quiet, snoring kind of breathing. She didn't seem like the kind of lady who would snore even a little, but apparently, she was. Bella and I had to cover our mouths so we didn't laugh. Lights were on next door at my house, though, and Jason and his friends were still shooting hoops even though it was all the way dark outside.

It was only two blocks to the cemetery.

Our neighborhood was built in the 1800s by silver miners. They must have been doing pretty well for themselves, because the houses were all large and none of them were the same. Some had towers on their sides like castles. Some had porches all the way around, and some had fancy wooden decoration all over. Some of them had been fixed up and looked perfect, like Bella's house, and a few looked like they were about to fall apart.

The neighborhood was on a hill—really it was on the slope of a smaller mountain. In some places the roads were steep. The houses looked charming during the day, but at night, they looked almost haunted. Maybe they were.

"This way," whispered Bella, hopping over a lower section of fence next to the large, ornate cemetery gates. My first foot landed in a muddy patch, and I tripped the rest of the way over the fence.

When we were inside, Bella pulled out her notebook. "Here's what we're looking for," she said. "Little spots of lights called orbs, full-body or partial-body apparitions, any strange shadows or any weird feelings."

"If we find any of these things, how will we know they are Helen?" I asked, rubbing my shoes into the grass to remove the mud.

"We'll ask," Bella said, turning on her flashlight and motioning for me to do the same. She stopped and sniffed the air. "Hmmm."

I sniffed, too. The air smelled spicy like the mountains and the wet grass and almost smoky at the same time. Bella leaned over close and whispered, "I smell mystery in the air—or maybe it's hamburgers. Let's go."

The cemetery was huge. It took up acres and acres, and there was no way we could cover every part of it in one night.

When we got far enough that we couldn't be seen from the street, Bella stopped. We stood in a small grove of trees. There were many little groves only a few trees deep that made for good hiding.

"Let's begin," she said.

I looked down and saw I was standing over the clenched-fist-gray grave of a woman named Maria Cosentino who was born in Italy in 1891 and died in Utah in 1975. Zuzu says that when you get a chill down your spine, that means someone is standing on your grave. I wondered if people really did know if you were standing on their grave. I wondered if somewhere out there Maria Cosentino was shivering. I shivered just thinking about it.

Bella turned out her flashlight and motioned for me to do the same. "Helen," she said to the night air. "Helen White, are you with us?" We both held our breath and listened. I heard crickets—lots of crickets and a bird, I wasn't sure what kind. "Helen, we are your friends. Are you there? Can you hear us?"

Suddenly, a creepy feeling crawled up my spine like someone was walking over my own grave. What if she answered? I wasn't sure I wanted to hear an answer. I listened in spite of myself. I couldn't help it.

"Hele . . ." Just then, there was the sound of swishing grass like someone was walking up behind us. I grabbed Bella's arm. We slowly turned around. No one was there. *Swish, swish, swish,* we heard it again, but again, no one was there. *Swish, swish, swish.* Bella and I stood frozen.

"Do you think . . . ," I whispered, when all of a sudden, a

brown rabbit hopped across my foot. I jumped and screamed. Bella screamed, too, but I don't think she even knew why we were screaming. The rabbit startled and hopped away, making the grass swish with each hop.

"Just a rabbit," said Bella. "You try."

"Um, Helen?" I said. I had never tried to talk to someone who was dead—not even my mom, at least not like that. I felt funny and uncomfortable. "Helen, are you in this graveyard?"

No answer.

"Let's go farther up the hill," said Bella.

We turned on our flashlights and headed up the surprisingly steep hill. From the top, a person could see the entire Salt Lake Valley lit up and sparkling in the night. We found a million things to put in the notebook because the entire place was filled with shadows and sounds and creepy feelings that were probably nothing, but definitely felt like something. We found another grove of trees and hid inside.

"Sadie," whispered Bella, "turn off your flashlight. I don't want you to scream."

"Okay," I said, feeling the sudden urge to do what she told me not to do. "Why?"

"Because we're being followed."

"What?" My heart gave an unnaturally huge jump. "Did you see something?" I asked, trying to quiet my breathing and my slamming heart.

"No, but I can hear it and feel it." Bella lifted her nose to the air like a dog picking up a scent.

"Is it . . . is it Helen?" I said, clutching Bella's arm hard.

"I don't know, but I think it may be more than one spirit."

"What?" I was even more alarmed. My knees felt wobbly and soft, like they couldn't support my weight much longer, and I was shaking—shaking hard.

"I'm not going to write it down here. I don't want to risk turning on the flashlight and scaring it away."

"*Us* scare *it?!*" I said so loudly that Bella shushed me.

"Earlier, I thought I saw some shadows that looked like human forms. Then as we climbed the hill, I kept seeing them out of the corner of my eye, but if I tried to look directly at them, they would run away before I could get a good look."

I glanced at Bella. She looked scared, too, but also exhilarated, like she had waited for this moment her entire life—like she was just about to hit the Everest summit. I felt just plain scared—knees-knocking scared.

"Do you think . . . ," I started.

"Don't move!" whispered Bella. "They're right behind us!"

I could hear my breath trembling and my whole body shook.

"When I say *three*," she said, "we'll turn around together and see if we can catch them. One, two—"

"Boo!"

Bella and I screamed and whipped around. There stood Jason and Derrick. Bella slugged Jason in the arm.

"You meanie!" she shouted. The boys laughed. I felt my heart begin to return to normal.

"What are you doing here?" asked Jason, who was holding

Bella's arm to steady her, which probably made her less steady than before.

"Us! What are you doing here?" asked Bella. "Anyway, it's none of your business."

"Well, it's none of your business why we're here, either," said Jason with a grin so big, I could clearly see it in the dark.

"Come on, Sadie, let's go home," Bella said, trying to sound annoyed but not pulling it off.

Jason linked arms with Bella and said in a fake English accent, "Then allow us to escort you home."

Bella beamed.

To my surprise, Derrick came up to me and offered his arm. I laughed and took it. He laughed, too.

Frozen-Ashes Black

"DO YOU EVER THINK ABOUT LIFE?" SAID Bella from her frozen-ashes-black bed.

"Sure," I said from my blanket bed on the floor.

"I mean, what it all means. Why we're here and what is going to happen to us?"

"Yeah, I think about it." At that moment, I thought of my mom. I thought of Sherrie and how the baby was coming soon. I wasn't sure I wanted to talk about this anymore.

"Sometimes I wonder . . . sometimes I wonder if my mom would be happier if I was more like my sisters. After my dad left, she sort of went into this thing where everything had to be perfect all the time and everything was about how things look. I think I don't fit. I mean, I don't think I'm the kind of girl she wanted."

"What do you think she wanted?"

"My sisters always had a million friends and loved to go

shopping with my mom and buy all the latest stuff. They were good at fitting in. They weren't . . . I don't know . . . different. I love art. I like music. I like doing my ghost research and writing. Someday I want to go to Paris and visit the Louvre. My mom would probably just want to go shopping and be annoyed at me for wanting to spend so much time looking at art that she thinks is weird or pointless, but I love it and I can't help it."

"I'm sure your mom likes you as much as your sisters," I said, but I thought I might be lying. I couldn't imagine anything worse than being a disappointment to your parents just because of who God made you to be. Maybe that was why it was hard to figure out where Bella came from—because she wasn't allowed to be that person.

"Someday, I am going to tell my mom off," she said. "Someday, I won't care what she thinks about me because I know the truth."

"What truth?"

"That I am Bella and there's nothing she can do about it."

"What do you think your mom will do?"

"Ground me, but I don't care. Grounding can't make a person be who they aren't. I wish she would just be happy to have me around. I wish she would just have fun with me like she did with my sisters."

I didn't know what to say. I didn't know if I should even say anything at all. "Well, I guess there's only one thing to do," I said finally.

"What?"

"Tell your mom off, run away to Paris with Jason and live happily ever after. He'll have fun with you."

"Sadie!" Bella laughed. So did I.

I yawned. It was quiet except for the crickets. I closed my eyes and saw Zuzu and her friends in the front yard, the cemetery and the million lights of the Salt Lake Valley.

Red-Bird Red

BELLA'S MOM MADE US PANCAKES with real maple syrup for breakfast. They were so good, I ate about a hundred and I wasn't sure I would ever want to eat again. I helped Bella do her morning chores so we could get them done fast. We wanted to read the day's entries before going to Grandma Brooks' to learn to crochet. We did the dishes, swept the floors, vacuumed and dusted. It seemed pointless to dust every surface in the living room and dining room when there wasn't a speck of dust in the whole house, but we did it anyway.

Zuzu was already outside with her friends, but excused herself and ran inside when she saw us coming.

"We had doughnuts for breakfast and they're all gone," said Zuzu.

"Big deal," I said. I wasn't sure I had the patience to deal with Zuzu. "We had homemade pancakes and real maple syrup."

"No fair!" she said, and stomped up the stairs.

Red rage swelled inside me. I knew I shouldn't get upset over Zuzu, well, just being Zuzu, but I felt like I couldn't take it today. I was glad Bella was there so at least I had one rational person my own age to hang around with. Zuzu apparently had the entire neighborhood to play with, and I felt annoyed that she had to spend so much time with us.

Bella and I fed Calamity and brought her up to Palace Beautiful. Zuzu was already waiting. We lit the candle and Bella read first.

October 9, 1918

Today at school all anyone talked about was influenza. Some kids said that the school might close until it goes away. Some said their parents think people are getting fanatical over nothing. Martha said her mother told her that there has always been influenza and no one has gotten upset about it before and that if people would only breathe deeply and remove their corsets, everything would be fine. Everyone laughed when she said it, but she didn't seem to understand why they were laughing.

Elaine Snow said some of the soldiers on both sides of the war are getting sick. Tyler Lund heard that people in other countries are getting sick.

I was glad to get home after school. When I got there, I picked up Anna and took her to the rocking chair. She loves to be rocked, and at the moment, I needed it, too. I needed to hold on to somebody to feel that I was home and safe and protected. Anna sucked her thumb and closed her eyes like a little baby—so content and warm. She has no idea what's lurking outside our house. As far as she's concerned, all is right with the world. Holding her in my arms with cooking smells coming from the kitchen, and Lizzy, Rachel and Freddy playing in the living room, I began to feel better, too.

It felt especially comforting when Father read scriptures to us tonight. I had a warm feeling in my soul that shut out war, sickness and everything else. I felt a swell of love for all the people in the room. In her evening prayer, Anna asked God to bless our family, the soldiers, the seagulls, the trees and horses (like she usually does), and then she went on to ask blessings on the silverware and the dishes, the curtains, the furniture and the knitting baskets. I could not help giggling. Father and Mother kept straight faces the whole time.

I finished the quilt I was making for Rachel's doll, and I gave it to her at bedtime. She loves it. She's embarrassed that she still sleeps with her doll, so she usually tucks it under her pillow to hide it. Tonight, she laid the doll next to her pillow and covered it with the quilt.

Good night.

—Helen

October 10, 1918

As of tomorrow all the schools and churches and public gatherings will be closed because of influenza. It *felt strange at school today. Everyone was sober and quiet. Mark and Lydia Judd were absent. No one wanted to ask why. When I got home, I still didn't ask. I didn't want to know.*

This evening Father told us he was closing his practice for a while. His clerk took sick Monday and has pulled through the worst of it, but Father said he did not want to take any chances. When he told us, he took little Freddy from Mother's arms and held him. I think Father is afraid of losing Freddy, too. Freddy started to cry and Father handed him back to Mother.

We read scriptures, and once again Anna blessed all the inanimate objects she could think of in our house. This time she asked blessing on the rugs, the quilts and her hair, which I suppose is not purely inanimate. Father and Mother kept a straight face. I do not think they were paying attention to the prayer. I think they were thinking about what will happen tomorrow when everything shuts down, and the day after that and the day after that. With those thoughts on a person's mind, it is easy to keep a straight face.

—Helen

Bella handed Zuzu the journal. I tried to imagine what it would feel like to have the flu take over the city. I felt a sickening chill run up and down my spine like electricity. I imagined it would feel like knowing that any day now, Sherrie was going to have the baby and everything would be wrong. Zuzu read:

October 11, 1918

Today, because there was no school, I went to Martha's house. We crocheted. Martha is making the prettiest yellow shawl. I think it will look like sunshine on her shoulders when it's finished. My red shawl is coming along nicely as well. The pattern is simple and fast, but it looks complicated.

While we worked, Paul took little pieces of newspaper, wadded them up and tossed them at us. We kept telling him to stop, but he would hide behind the sofa or in the living room doorway or anywhere we wouldn't see him and throw them from there. I kept having to pick them out of my shawl. I'm just glad they were only crumpled paper and not spit wads. He and Charlie throw spit wads at us at school. I guess plain, dry crumpled paper is Paul's way of being nice.

Finally, after Martha told her mom on him about a hundred times, and after he denied it a hundred times, Mrs. Phelps caught him in the act and he was sent outside. He kept looking in the front window at Martha and me and sticking his tongue out. Martha and I just rolled our eyes and tried to ignore him.

Martha crochets faster than just about anyone I know. She will be done with her shawl in no time. I'm not as fast as her.

When I got home, mother made meat pies with potatoes and gravy. It was so nice. It definitely feels like autumn now, and Mother's meat pies always make me feel cozy in cool weather. It is raining outside and a bit chilly. I like chilly this time of year. It is not freezing, but cold enough to snuggle down into the covers.

Good night.

—Helen

P.S. I saw Lizzy and Matthew Stoker kiss by the sycamore tree.

"Gross!" said Zuzu.

"Oh, be quiet," I said. Zuzu kept reading.

October 12, 1918

Today it almost snowed at our house. The mountains are completely dusted, and I think it might have snowed as low as Fort Douglas. It's still raining here in the lower elevations, but it will be snowing soon enough.

Father wrapped the little sycamore tree in the front yard with rags and twine to protect it from the winter cold. Anna and Rachel planted it in the spring and they still care for it like it was a baby. Anna used to cry when it would rain because the tree had to be out in the weather all by itself. We tried to explain to her that trees don't mind—they like rain—but she wouldn't have any of it. Father said someday it will be big enough to touch my bedroom window. I can't imagine it.

"Hey!" said Zuzu. "It does! That's your room, Sadie!"

"Zuzu, keep reading," I said.

Anna was fretful today, so I tended her for Mother. The only thing that seemed to cheer Anna up was for me to play her version of peekaboo. She hides behind the sofa while I work on my crocheting and act like I don't know where she is. Then she jumps out and I pretend to be startled. She laughs and laughs and does it over and over again until I can't stand it anymore. I'm certain she could play that game an entire week without a break and not get tired of it.

Freddy is a rosy, fat baby. He has the chubbiest cheeks and two big dimples in the center of each. He is so happy, especially when Rachel tends him. She seems just as happy with him as he is with her. I still won't hold him, though, unless I have to. I know as soon as I let my guard down, it will all fall apart. I must admit, only in the privacy of my journal, that I am growing a little fond of him—a little. To me that is all the more reason to leave him to Rachel and Mother.

Mother is up and around now. She smiles and sings while she works. Rachel smiles and sings as she tends Freddy. Lizzy smiles and sings as she thinks of Matthew Stoker. I told Lizzy I saw her and Matthew kiss yesterday. She denied it, but I saw it with my own two eyes. Later, she admitted it. She smiled so big, all of her teeth showed and little crinkles formed at the edges of her eyes.

Father doesn't smile and sing when he is home. Things are weighing heavy on his mind. He won't talk about it, but I'm sure it is some turn of the war, influenza or his practice. Whatever it is, he is trying to keep it from troubling his home. I think it is worse when he pretends nothing is bothering him when something clearly is. I am *pretending I don't notice his troubles just like I pretend I don't know that Anna is hiding behind the couch. It is easier to do when everyone else is so content and the mountains are sprinkled with white and the air is cool and clean.*

—Helen

Zuzu handed the journal to me. I realized that in all the years we had come to Utah to visit Grandma Brooks, I had never noticed the snow creeping down the mountains. Houston doesn't have snow—or mountains. I realized that in only a few months, I would have to wear gloves and a hat, and for the first time, I'd see the snow inching its way into the valley.

I read:

October 13, 1918

Today is Sunday and there was no church. It felt so strange to just stay home. I watched out the window and it felt strange again to see the streets empty. Usually on Sunday everyone is going to or from church and paying visits to neighbors. Today, I saw only a few people out the window, and they walked hurriedly, wearing gauze masks.

Father had us study our scriptures extra today to make up for not having church. I spent the day reading, resting and playing peekaboo with Anna. For some reason, all that resting made me feel more tired than if I'd gone to church. I am getting a little sick of being at home all the time. I hope they open the schools next week.

This afternoon I was in my Palace Beautiful and I was almost discovered! Mother came to the attic to get something. I sat as still and quiet as I could. I heard her footsteps walking around the attic, but she didn't notice the little crawl space opening. It was a close call!

This afternoon, from the attic window, I saw two white quarantine cards in house windows down the street.

Tonight Anna swore at the dinner table. She said, "Could you please pass the damn corn?" Lizzy, Rachel and I burst out laughing. Mother told Anna she had said a bad word, and Anna started to cry because she didn't know that what she had said was bad. Mother and Father didn't laugh, but I could tell they wanted to.

—Helen

October 14, 1918

The sun came out today and most of the snow on the mountains melted. We are still allowed to go out and be with friends, but by law, because of the influenza, we have to wear a gauze mask when we are in public and we have to avoid crowds. All of the shops and businesses are closed or on limited hours just so people can get the necessities. There is not much to do, and when the weather is fine, it is hard to be at home all day.

After chores, I was allowed to go to Martha's. We took out our crocheting and sat in her parlor and worked. Martha's shawl is coming so fast. She only has a few more rows. Mine is much slower.

While I was at the Phelpses' house, Matthew Stoker

paid a visit to Lizzy. Now it's like Lizzy's face is stuck in a kind of permanent blushy grin. I hope I don't look that silly and swoony if I ever decide to get a beau.

Mother, Lizzy and I harvested some of the vegetables in the garden and spent the evening preserving. I did some more decorating in my Palace Beautiful. I hung the last of the year's flowers upside down to dry and I painted the words Palace Beautiful *over the doorway. I pinned two brass lion buttons on either side of the words just like the lions in* The Pilgrim's Progress *that guard the doorway to the Palace Beautiful. I think it looks quite nice.*

—Helen

I closed the book and blew out the candle.

"She's going to get the flu and she's going to die!" said Zuzu.

"I don't know," said Bella. "We tried to contact her in the cemetery and we didn't get a response."

"What?!" said Zuzu, flinging her arms in the air and almost hitting us both. "When did you go to the cemetery? How come I wasn't invited! Life is so unfair!"

"Zuzu, it was when I slept over at Bella's. Now, be quiet or someone will hear you."

"It's no fair! No one ever lets me do anything fun!" she whispered. "If I was in Jennifer Meyer's family . . ."

"That's enough!" I said. "That's exactly why we didn't take you!" The red rage boiled higher and I wanted to tell her to get out or hit her or something, but neither would help, so

I swallowed hard and tried to make the anger go away. It didn't work. I think Zuzu knew she had crossed the line, because she put her hands back in her lap and was quiet.

"Anyway," said Bella, "we didn't find her in the cemetery."

"That doesn't mean she's alive," said Zuzu. "I think she is going to die for sure. Why else would this room—journal and all—be left just like it was way back then?"

"I'll be right back," I said. I went downstairs and retrieved the big yellow phone book and brought it up to the attic. "Let's look up Denton and White, Helen's dad's law practice."

I flipped through the pages. There were about thirty pages of lawyer ads. Some of the ads were big and had photos of wrecked cars or of barred doors like a jail, and some were smaller with just the name and phone number. I had no idea one city could have so many lawyers. We all looked through the pages so we wouldn't miss it in the jumble of ads.

"Look, there it is," I said, pointing to a square ad that said, "Denton and White, working for you."

"It's still here and it's close enough to walk," said Bella. "Let's go check it out and see if we can get any information about Helen and her family."

"Let's go now!" said Zuzu.

"We told Grandma Brooks we'd go to her house and learn to crochet. Let's do that, then go."

"I want to make a red shawl like Helen's," said Bella. "I think we should make it together and keep it here in Palace Beautiful."

"That sounds nice," I said.

"That sounds boring to me," said Zuzu.

"What?" I said, raising an eyebrow at her.

"Fine. It sounds great."

We left Palace Beautiful, went downstairs and told Sherrie where we were going. I had to wake her up to tell her.

The air was still and hot. It quivered and pulsed and radiated summer. The trees stood motionless—preserving their energy in the heat. Kids playing in front yards moved slowly and heavily.

"Hello, girls!" called Grandma Brooks from the rose-bushes in her front yard.

"Hi, Grandma," I said.

"I was just wishing for some company," she said. "I tried a new banana bread recipe this morning. Come on in."

Bella's face brightened and she marched in right after Grandma. As soon as we were inside, Bella breathed in deeply and exhaled long and slow.

"Grandma Brooks," said Bella, "we're here to learn to crochet."

"Well, that's just fine!" said Grandma, looking very pleased. "I'll get my yarn." She disappeared upstairs.

Zuzu looked at the wall next to the window that was lined with old books. She fingered them and blew dust off their covers.

I took a seat on the old velvet sofa and Bella sat next to me. A minute later, Grandma Brooks came downstairs carrying an enormous oil-slick-black garbage bag stuffed so full, it barely fit down the stairway. With the bag slung over her shoulders, she looked a bit like Santa Claus.

She opened the bag and said, "Choose a color."

Bella dove in first. The bag was full of yarn of every size, shape and color. Bella pulled out three large balls of red yarn just the color of the birds that filled the branches of the mourning apple tree.

"I want to make a red shawl," she said.

"Well, okay," said Grandma Brooks. "I think I'll teach you how to make granny squares then. To make a shawl, you can make a lot of squares and sew them together any way you want."

Zuzu reached in next and found a ball of bright hello-there! pink. I found some directly-at-the-sun white.

Grandma Brooks handed us each a metal crochet hook and began to teach the stitches. I struggled. Bella seemed to get it right away, and Zuzu seemed more interested in the banana bread in the kitchen.

"When I was your age, we had to crochet, sew and knit," said Grandma.

"We know," said Zuzu. "We read about it in the journal."

I flashed Zuzu a fierce look that shut her mouth instantly.

"Did you always live here?" Bella asked quickly.

"Almost," said Grandma Brooks. "Well, I was born here, but moved away when I got married. Two years later, my parents died and we inherited the house. I've lived here ever since."

"How did your parents die?" asked Bella.

I realized I didn't even know the answer to that question, and they were my family.

"They got pneumonia, and they died a week apart."

"Do you . . . ," Zuzu started. She looked at me and I could tell she was going to ask about something in the journal, but didn't want me to get mad at her. She thought for a minute and then said, "Do you remember the influenza thing in 1918?"

"No, I can't say that I do," Grandma Brooks replied. "I was only four at the time. I do remember that as I got older, just about everyone I knew had lost a family member to it. I'm glad I don't remember. It must have been a terrible time."

"It was," said Zuzu, staring at her shoes. She didn't even notice my "be quiet" glare.

The clock on the mantel dinged a quarter past, then half past, then quarter till, then the hour.

"That's enough!" said Zuzu, dropping her work. "I'm starving!"

"Zuzu!" I said.

"Let me have a look at that, Zuzu," said Grandma Brooks. "You did a fine job for a first try."

"That's just a nice way to say it stinks!" said Zuzu. "I hate crocheting!"

I elbowed her in the ribs.

"Stop it, Sadie!" she said.

"I like crocheting," said Bella, holding up two perfect red-bird-red granny squares.

"Very good, Bella. You're a natural!" said Grandma Brooks. Bella beamed with pride.

"Yours looks pretty good, too, Sadie."

"Thank you." She always thought you did great, even when you didn't.

We went to the kitchen and ate banana bread while Grandma Brooks took our yarn and hooks and put them in individual freezer bags to take home. When we finished, we thanked Grandma and said good-bye.

Zuzu and I put our freezer bags away at our house, and Bella took her crocheting to her house, and we set off to find Denton and White.

Baked-Mud Brown

ALL THE STREETS IN SALT LAKE CITY are arranged in a grid pattern. They run north to south and east to west and they are numbered from the center of town. That is one thing I love about Salt Lake City—even if a person doesn't know exactly where they are going, if they have an address, they can find it.

"The phone book says the law firm is at 900 East, 127 South. It's only a few blocks away," said Bella, who knew all the streets and the grid very well.

When we got close to the office, I began to feel a fluttery feeling in my stomach. I wasn't sure if the building would be a modern replacement for the one Helen's dad had worked at or if it was the actual building. As soon as I saw it, I knew it was clearly the exact same building. It was an old baked-mud-brown mansion turned into several business offices.

In the middle of our neighborhood of big houses, there

were several mansions. Most of them had been turned into something else, like private schools or law offices. This one had a pretty tower on the side with windows that were curved around it. It was shaded by two enormous sycamore trees. It was tall and had a pointed roof and a pointed tower and pointed gabled windows that all made the building look even taller. A wooden sign in the front yard read, MILLER REALTORS, INC.; COPY SOLUTIONS; DENTON AND WHITE, ATTORNEYS AT LAW.

A chilly thrill ran across my skin and sank deep into my stomach as I imagined that Helen herself might have been in this same yard playing with her sisters many years ago. If Bella had felt that thrill, she probably would have said it was Helen's ghost saying hello, and maybe that's exactly what it was.

"This is it!" said Bella.

Zuzu, who was standing between Bella and me, took both of our hands in hers and gave them a squeeze like a little mother.

"Maybe Helen is here right now," said Bella.

"Maybe," I said, feeling the icy chill run up my spine.

"Yeah," said Zuzu, almost whispering. "Maybe she's the secretary."

"Jeez, Zuzu!" I said, rolling my eyes.

"What?" said Zuzu. She dropped my hand but kept Bella's, and we walked in the front door.

"But maybe," Bella began, her honey-black eyes shining, "maybe her ghost walks the halls and wails for the loss of her father. Well, maybe they both wail."

We followed several modern-looking signs upstairs and through halls until we came to Denton and White.

"Can I help you?" asked a secretary who was too young to be Helen herself.

"We were wondering . . . ," I started. I suddenly realized I had no idea what to say. "We were wondering about the history of this place."

"What do you mean?" asked the secretary.

"This building," I said. "This law practice."

"Oh." She looked a little confused. I couldn't blame her. I guess kids don't usually wonder about the history of businesses. "It was started by Fredrick Denton and Samuel White way back a long time ago. I think it was around 1905, give or take a decade."

"Fredrick—Freddy!" whispered Zuzu.

"Fredrick was the Denton, not the White," I whispered.

"I mean, I bet that's where Freddy got his name," she said, poking me in the ribs. "Jeez!"

"There's a couple of photos on the wall over there," said the secretary.

We followed her manicured finger until we saw a wall of old photos. Most of them were of the neighborhood and the mansion back when it was new, but in one of the photos, Fredrick and Samuel were shaking hands in front of the building. Helen's dad looked just like he did in the family picture. Maybe a little bit younger, but I recognized him right away.

"Can I ask why you all are so interested in this place?"

"We live in the house that Samuel White lived in back then, and we were just curious about his family," said Zuzu. I was impressed that she could be so straightforward without confessing everything.

"Well, I don't really know anything about him or his family, but you might check with Sally Kimball. She is Mr. Denton's daughter and she still lives in town. I don't have her number, but I think she is still around."

"Sally Kimball," Bella said to herself. She took the zebra-striped notebook out of her purse and scribbled the name.

"Did you ever meet any of the Whites?" asked Bella.

"I can't say that I did," answered the secretary. "I do know that Mr. White didn't work here long. I think he had some sort of tragedy in his family and they left town. He and Mr. Denton were good friends, and Denton kept his name in the practice to honor him. I'm not completely sure, though."

"Thank you for your time," I said.

"I hope it helps," said the secretary, returning to her desk.

"We've got to find Sally Kimball," I said when we were back out on the lawn.

"I can't today. I have to go home and do chores," Bella told us.

I thought about her immaculate house and wondered what kind of chores she could possibly do for so many hours a day.

We had left the house spotless only a few hours before. I felt sorry for her. I did my share of the housework, but I would also get to spend the afternoon playing with Calamity and painting.

"Tomorrow," I said, and we walked home, baking in the mountain sun.

September Orange

THE MORNING SUN TIPTOED ACROSS my room. The air was so still that even the sycamore didn't move. I sat on my bed petting Calamity. She was so tiny and warm. She rolled around on my quilt and batted my fingertips. I was trying to paint her portrait, but I couldn't get her to stay still long enough.

I tried a different paintbrush, but Calamity just batted at the old one and got mourning-dove-gray paint on her tiny paws.

I had already been to Bella's that morning to see if she could read the journal. Her mom had answered and said she couldn't come over because she had to do chores. I decided that since she couldn't come over, I would paint instead.

"Sadie!" Zuzu shouted, bursting into my room.

"What?" I said in a tone that would make it clear that her barging in without knocking was very annoying.

"Helen. She's dead!"

"What? You read the rest of the journal without us?!" I pushed my paints aside and jumped off my bed.

"No! Of course not! I heard her!"

"What? Where? What are you talking about?"

"In the attic! I heard her! She was a ghost!"

"Zuzu, I . . . what?" I said.

"Can't talk, have to get Bella!" Zuzu turned and bolted out the door.

I picked up my paints, dumped out the water and had just cleaned the brushes when Zuzu and Bella appeared in my doorway.

"Come on!" Zuzu whispered so loudly that she almost shouted.

"I thought you were supposed to be doing chores," I said to Bella. Her cheeks flushed and she looked at the floor.

"No," she said.

I could tell she was lying. She must have snuck out of her house.

"Come on!" whined Zuzu. She pulled Bella and me by the hands up the attic steps.

"There!" she said, panting and wiping her damp golden curls from her forehead.

"I don't hear anything," I said.

"I heard her!" Zuzu said, stamping her Sunday shoes on the bare wood floor.

"Was it the kids playing down the street?" I asked.

"Of course not! I'm not stupid!"

"What was it, then?" I said, crossing my arms skeptically like I was from the cabbage patch.

"It was a voice. She was singing."

"What was she singing?" I asked, dropping my arms in accidental interest.

"I don't know, but somehow, I knew the song. Maybe she has haunted us always and we were meant to come to her house and find her."

"What did the song sound like?" Bella asked.

"I can't explain it. It was just a song and she was singing it and I knew it! Listen!" ordered Zuzu.

We all froze and stood as still as we possibly could. I heard the kids playing down the street, a faraway airplane and some birds. I heard the dishwasher from downstairs, but I didn't hear any singing.

"You sure it wasn't someone outside?" I asked.

"Positive! I looked out every window and no one was out, but I heard it as plain as day! I think we need to find Sally Kimball right now!" said Zuzu. "Let's go!"

"Wait," I said. "Let's read the journal for today and see if we hear any singing while we are here. Bella, do you need to go back home and finish your chores like your mom said this morning?"

"I'm finished," she said, looking at her feet.

"You won't get in trouble?" I asked.

"No," she said so firmly that she sounded like she was from the cabbage patch. I hoped she was right, but I wasn't sure I believed her.

We lit the candle and Bella read first.

October 15, 1918

I have to admit, it is kind of nice to have no school for now. I don't like people to be sick, but when I'm home, I can sometimes forget about influenza.

I finished my shawl and it looks beautiful! I finished it just in time, because the weather has turned and it is cold. Lizzy is starting one now. Hers is a rusty orange color. She is using a pattern she got from Mrs. Phelps last year. I think it will be pretty, but I wonder how long it will take her. Lizzy likes to sew, but hates to crochet.

Martha came over after chores. She is crazy about little Freddy. She kept asking to hold him every second. He likes her, too. She said she doesn't understand why I don't hold him or play with him. If she had to think about making his little burial gown and seeing him in a tiny little casket, she would understand sure enough. I have to admit, though, he is a sweet little boy.

Anna loves having Rachel, Lizzy and me home from school. She keeps running from Lizzy to Rachel to me and back again, saying, "Boo!" Then we pretend to be startled. She is such a funny little thing. We couldn't send her out to play because it was raining, so we had to do our work all day with her saying, "Boo!" every few seconds. I'm surprised she hasn't lost her voice.

I am in my Palace Beautiful right now. I can hear the rain on the roof and feel the chill of autumn. It feels nice.

—Helen

October 18, 1918

I didn't write much this week because there was nothing to say. Every day was the same—eat, sleep, chores and rain. At first it was nice, but now it's hard to be cooped up all day with the same people. Martha had a cold and couldn't come over, so I spent the week playing peekaboo with Anna, and arguing with Lizzy and Rachel. They can be so difficult sometimes. Mother threatened that if she has to scold us one more time, she will let Father do it. He can be much more harsh than Mother, so we tried our best to behave. It is so hard, though.

I haven't been outside because of the rain, but I imagine there are white quarantine cards in front windows everywhere. I can see the cemetery from the attic window. Every day there are several burials. It seems like the number is growing every day. Since all public gatherings are prohibited, they can't even have proper funerals. The cemetery is filled with grave diggers and caskets.

I hate this influenza. I am tired of being stuck at home. I want things to go back to normal. Father says he thinks it won't be much longer. I've been sitting at my window watching the rain. Every once in a while, I'll see someone walk down the street. Most people are stuck inside like I am. When they go out, they have to wear a gauze mask. It's like a walking reminder that things are unsure and uncertain and scary.

Freddy and Anna seem to be the only ones who are happy lately. The other day Freddy smiled at Mother.

She heard him cooing in his cradle, and when she went to get him, he looked at her and smiled. Anna came up behind her and said, "Boo!" It scared Freddy and he cried, but he has since given a smile to just about everyone in our family—everyone except me. I've stayed away. I don't want a smile from him.

—Helen

Bella handed the book to me. Calamity jumped off my lap and curled up in the corner as I read:

October 20, 1918

We just had another day without church, another day of bickering and another day of rain. This can't go on much longer. Yesterday, Martha couldn't come over, so I took my shawl and a book and spent hours hiding out in Palace Beautiful. I've had enough of all of this. I'm ready to go back to school. I don't even feel like writing in my journal anymore. It feels like real life has stopped and the world is paralyzed. I don't know how much longer we can stay frozen in waiting.

—Helen

October 21, 1918

Today the sun came out and it almost felt like summer again. Anna spent the morning and afternoon chasing butterflies in the backyard and Lizzy, Rachel and I didn't have to spend the whole day playing peekaboo. Thank heavens!

Martha and I took a walk around the neighborhood.
We had to wear masks. We saw four new quarantine
cards and almost no people. Everyone in the neighborhood
was inside. It felt strange.

After our walk I went to Martha's house. Paul and
Charlie were in the front yard hitting the apple tree with a
rake handle. All of the good apples had already been
picked. They were knocking down the rotten, smelly ones
half eaten by birds and bugs. They threatened to throw
them at us, but we got inside in time to avoid it. I wasn't
sure if they really would or not, but I didn't want to
find out.

When I got home at dinnertime, I felt so much better.
It was nice to have a break from being home all the time.
—Helen

I handed the book to Zuzu. I glanced around the room
and tried to imagine Helen hiding out here. Zuzu read:

October 25, 1918
Life is more of the same. I don't have anything to
write. The sun stayed out most of the week, but each day
seems like the same day over and over. We are just
waiting for influenza to run its course and leave. It seems
to be getting worse, and we don't know when we will be
able to get back to school. I'm almost getting used to it. I
just do my chores and try not to think about things. It gets
easier to forget every day. It feels like influenza was
always here and I was always stuck at home. It feels like

I was never at church being pelted with crab apples by Paul and Charlie. I'm just tired lately and I still don't feel like writing.

  —Helen

November 1, 1918

  School is still out, white cards are still in windows, the cemetery is still crowded and I am still home. There is no end in sight. All I want to do is sleep. Father says to keep our chins up and that this too shall pass. I'm starting to think he is just plain wrong. What if it stays like the war? What if it never ends? What if this is now the normal way of life? Halloween was yesterday, but because of influenza, everyone had to stay home—where we have been for weeks now.

  —Helen

"No trick-or-treating?" said Zuzu, closing the book. "That stinks!"

"I can't believe this all really happened and it happened right here," I said. I reached over and blew out the candle. The little smoke fingers wrapped around the room and we sat silently.

"I would hate to be living back then," said Zuzu. "No trick-or-treating!"

"There's worse things than that, Zuzu," said Bella. "I wish I *had* lived back then. I wish I was in the White family." She picked at a loose thread on her just-before-the-dawn-black skirt.

"Even if you had to skip Halloween?" asked Zuzu skeptically.

Bella just looked at the floor and didn't answer.

"Even if they are going to die?" I asked.

"Being loved and enjoyed like the White kids are is better than living a long time and being extra."

"What's extra?" asked Zuzu. Bella didn't answer and neither did I.

"Listen," said Zuzu.

"For what?" I asked. Calamity crawled off Zuzu's lap and curled up in mine. I could feel her purring.

"The singing, jeez!" said Zuzu, rolling her eyes and crossing her arms hard.

We all sat quietly. After a minute, Bella said, "I don't hear any singing."

"Me neither," said Zuzu.

"Me neither," I said, too.

"We've got to find Helen once and for all!" insisted Zuzu, setting the journal back in its place of honor.

"I'll be right back," I said, getting up and leaving the attic. I came back up a few minutes later with the phone book. We flipped through all the Kimballs in the area. There were a lot. We finally came across a Ben and Sally, and they lived in our neighborhood. Zuzu wrote down the address and we left.

We passed Bella's house, which was closed and dark and perfect as usual. Bella stopped and looked for a moment. Then she continued walking.

"I think I am going to open my curtains from now on," she said, looking back at her bedroom window.

Zuzu climbed resolutely up the front steps of the house we hoped was Sally Kimball's. She rang the doorbell and we waited.

"Can I help you?" A middle-aged woman with long, graying hair and a September-orange dress opened the door a crack.

"We are looking for a Sally Kimball," said Zuzu.

"I'm her daughter," said the woman.

"Is she home?" asked Bella, almost hiding behind Zuzu and me.

"Actually, she passed away last month," said the woman, opening the door a bit wider.

"Oh," said Bella, dropping her eyes to the concrete porch.

"We were looking for Sally because we were told she might have known the White family that lived in our house before us," I said.

"Sure, she knew the Whites. Do you mean Samuel and Mary?"

"Yes!" shouted Zuzu.

"We were wondering what happened to them—if you know," I said, wishing I felt as bold as Zuzu acted.

"Oh, I don't know. They moved away long before I was born. My mother used to tell me stories of her childhood, though, where she played with one of the White girls— Elizabeth, I think, was her name."

"Lizzy!" said Zuzu.

"Yes, Lizzy. That's it."

"Well, do you know where we could find out if any of them are still alive?"

"I don't know. We are going through my mother's things right now. If you leave your phone number, I can call you if I find anything." She looked amused and smiled at us.

Bella scribbled our phone numbers on a scrap of paper from her zebra-striped notebook.

"Thank you for your help," I said.

We walked home, not knowing anything more than we had before, but feeling on the edge of knowing absolutely everything.

Spontaneous-Combustion Scarlet

WHEN WE GOT HOME, SHERRIE WAS sitting on the front porch with a glass of water in her hand, burrowing her bare feet in the cool grass.

"Shouldn't you be napping or something—you know, the baby?" I asked.

"Probably, but I just can't stand being cooped up all day. I had to come out and get some fresh air. The baby's busy and it's hard to rest."

"Can I . . . can I feel the baby?" Bella asked, blushing.

"Of course you can," said Sherrie.

Bella sat down beside her and put her hand on Sherrie's stomach. A huge smile suddenly burst over Bella's face. "I feel it!" she said. "I feel the baby!"

"Pretty amazing, isn't it?" Sherrie said. She leaned back on her hands for balance. She looked so uncomfortable, I felt sorry for her. "I think it's one of the strangest and most wonderful feelings in the world to have a baby growing inside your own body."

"Sherrie!" said Zuzu. She was embarrassed by any talk about bodies. She had found out last year where babies come from—and I don't mean the Great Dog or the cabbage patch—and still hadn't come to grips with it. Now she thought anything anyone said about babies and bodies in the same sentence was mortifying.

"It's all right, Sugar. It's just part of life," Sherrie said.

"Part of YOUR life—not mine!" Zuzu said. "GROSS!"

"What do you think is the most important thing in life?" asked Bella, leaning back on her hands just like Sherrie.

"Well," Sherrie said. "I guess love—and the pursuit of beauty."

"Me, too," Bella said. "And longing."

"Longing?" Sherrie asked.

"Yeah," said Bella. Her eyes pointed to the sycamore tree but looked like they were far, far away.

"For beauty?" asked Sherrie.

"Yes, and . . ."

"And what?" I asked.

"Jason Prince," said Bella, her face turning spontaneous-combustion scarlet. She dropped her eyes to the ground and smiled so big, she almost didn't look like Bella. Or maybe she looked exactly like Bella.

I accidentally let out a giggle. Bella followed and Sherrie, too. Zuzu just rolled her eyes and sat down in the grass. Jason and Derrick were down the street shooting hoops just like the other day. And just like the other day, they stopped playing for a moment and waved at us. Jason called, "Hi, Bella." Bella waved back, but could hardly raise her eyes off the lawn.

"Hark! The handsome prince acknowledges his fair princess," said Sherrie, and we all crumpled into a fit of laughter—even Zuzu.

Dad drove up. He got out of the car carrying two pizza boxes.

"Lunch!" he called. "Looks like a good day for a picnic." He placed the pizzas next to Sherrie and went inside to get a blanket. He spread it out on the grass, and we all ate pizza and laughed.

Half an hour later, Bella's mom pulled up in her driveway and Bella stopped laughing. Her mom noticed Bella in our front yard and came marching over with her hands on her hips.

"Kristin!" she said so sharply that even Dad jumped. "What did I tell you before I left?"

Bella stared blankly at the ground. "To . . . to clean my room?"

"No! I told you to stay home while I'm gone so I know where you are."

"We can keep an eye on her, Holly," said Sherrie. "She's been with the girls all morning."

"Is that so?" said Holly, raising her eyebrows and glaring at Bella. "I'm so sorry. You all have enough to worry about without having to take care of Kristin."

"Really," Sherrie told her. "She's no trouble at all. We all like having her over."

"That's nice of you to say," said Holly.

"Mom, the Brookses were all home and it was fine with them. I feel better here than all alone in the house all day. It's just that . . ."

Holly looked at Bella sharply. Bella got up and brushed off her skirt and followed her mom next door. She looked back just as they reached her front door. "Thanks for the pizza!" she called.

"Good thing Bella never met Jennifer Meyer's family. She'd never want to go home again," said Zuzu.

"I think, to Bella, we probably are Jennifer Meyer's family." I glanced at their large house. Every time I'd seen it, all the blinds had been closed and all the windows shut—like someone was holed up inside and hiding. I thought about Bella saying that she wanted to keep her curtains open from now on. I hoped she would.

That evening, I went upstairs and took my mother's photograph out of the shoe box and pinned it up in Palace Beautiful next to the photo of Helen's family. It looked just right.

I painted a picture from Helen's family photo. Since it was an old photograph, it was all black and white, but I painted the colors that I imagined were there, like bonnie blue, funny yellow and star white. I blushed all the cheeks, colored all the eyes and tinted all the lips.

I used a teeny-tiny brush to get the details of Helen's father's mustache, Freddy's little slippers and Rachel's half-closed eyes. I made each feather in Helen's mother's hat. I painted Lizzy's crochet lace gloves, and Helen's long curls.

When it was finished, I blew on the picture to help it dry faster. Things dried faster in Utah than they did in Texas. I covered the room entrance with boxes and closed up my paint box. I hoped Bella had a Palace Beautiful in her home where she could feel happy, too.

Sweet-Butter Peach

"**S**HERRIE," I SAID, CLIMBING ONTO HER bed that evening, "who was your mom?"

Sherrie always said she was an orphan. Her mom died the year before she met Dad, and her father died several years before that. She didn't talk about them much.

"Her name was Olivia Marie Davies."

"What was she like?"

"She was little even when she was a grown woman, and she loved riding horses."

"What was she like—I mean as a mom?"

Sherrie pulled herself up with her arms to a sitting position. Her sweet-butter-peach robe clung to her round stomach and I could see the baby move and shift inside her.

"She was strict, but I'm sure she meant well. It was just her way."

"How?"

Sherrie sighed. It wasn't just the baby that made her uncomfortable. I realized for the first time that maybe she didn't talk about her mom because they didn't get along.

"She did her best. My father drank a lot and she had to run the ranch herself. It was a tough job. I'm an only child, so I had a lot of responsibility. She and I took care of the ranch together."

"Did you . . . did you get along?"

"I loved her and she loved me. We had our differences, but . . ." She stopped there. "Put your hand here," she said, placing my hands on her swollen belly. I felt the baby rolling and kicking. "Sometimes I wonder if this little one is like my mother—kicking and squirming and raring to go. My mother was a spitfire and always restless. She liked to do things her way and only her way and didn't let anyone else tell her different."

Sherrie took in a long breath and let it out in tiny puffs. She was having a contraction.

"Are you all right?"

"Yes. It's just that I don't think this baby wants to wait around very much longer. It's not time right now, though."

"How do you know?"

"I guess it's just a feeling."

"Are you still scared?"

"Yes."

"Me, too."

Sherrie wrapped her arms around me and held me for a long time.

Desolate-Hour Gray

THE NEXT MORNING BELLA SHOWED up as early as usual, but she looked like she does when she's in her own house. The corners of her mouth drooped and her shoulders slumped. She moved slowly up the attic steps.

As I followed her up the steps, I felt a red rage igniting in my stomach. I was angry that Bella got treated so badly at home. I was angry that she loved her mother and her mother treated her like she was a terrible inconvenience—an extra person.

None of us spoke as Bella lit the candle and Zuzu picked up the journal. She handed it to Bella, who began to read:

November 2, 1918
   I hardly know what day it is anymore. All the days seem to blend together in one exhausting blur. I snapped at Anna today. She wouldn't stop jumping out from behind the couch and yelling, "Boo!" I couldn't take it

anymore, and I yelled at her to stop and said that everyone knows she's there and we are just pretending to be surprised. She cried and cried, and I tried to feel bad, but I'm just too tired.

I've stopped hoping for school to start and I've stopped hoping influenza will go away just like I've stopped hoping the war will end. It now just feels like part of life instead of something separate and different.

After lunch, I fell asleep in Palace Beautiful with my shawl around my shoulders. I'm so glad I finished it when I did. It feels like the only bright thing in the house. The shawl is vivid, soft and warm and we are all dull and tired and every day is just like the one before.

—Helen

November 3, 1918

This morning, Lizzy and I couldn't stop fighting, so I went upstairs and spent the rest of the day in Palace Beautiful.

Freddy was fretful and I could hear him crying all day. I don't feel like writing anymore.

—Helen

Bella handed the journal to me and I read:

November 4, 1918

Anna spent the entire morning pulling at the fringe on my red shawl. Even she is getting tired now. We sent her out to play in the backyard. After a few minutes, we checked on her and she was curled up under the apple tree. She looked like she was asleep, but she wasn't. She sighed and looked so mournful, I took her in my arms and wrapped her in my shawl. She smiled, but I could tell she was getting worn out, too. I took her inside and read her a story, and that picked her up a little. I have almost forgotten what it feels like to not be tired.

—Helen

November 5, 1918

This afternoon, the best thing happened. Mother said she decided we needed a party. She took some pies and some preserves from the larder and set them out. She dressed a roast with carrots, cabbage and onions. She told Rachel and me to peel and boil some potatoes. Anna was set to work gathering sticks and dried flowers and whatever else she could find for a table centerpiece. Mother baked white biscuits and a pound cake.

When the baking was under way, Lizzy, Anna, Rachel and I decorated the table and the dining room with crepe paper streamers and ribbon roses. Rachel made some larger roses from strips of fabric from the ragbag and placed them in the center of the table. Anna finished off the centerpiece with a pile of twigs and a few small stones. They looked funny, but Anna was so proud that we thought maybe they didn't look so bad after all.

We went to our rooms and dressed in our Sunday clothes and fixed our hair. When all was ready, Mother called us down.

I had never seen such a beautiful table! It was such a feast! My sisters and my mother looked beautiful, and my father and even Freddy looked handsome in their Sunday best.

We ate and laughed and talked and laughed and ate some more. When we were finished, it was late and we felt full, sleepy and satisfied.

Father read to us and Anna fell asleep in my lap smiling.

—Helen

"I want to have a party like that," said Zuzu, "only with no onions. Gross!" She took the journal out of my hands and read:

November 7, 1918

Mother isn't feeling well. I'm scared. She went to the Moodys' a few days ago to drop off some bread and apple butter. Since then, the Moodys have had influenza. I'm afraid Mother has it.

She seemed to be fine this morning, maybe just a little tired. This afternoon she went down for a rest, and when she woke up, she had a fever. Father says it might be just a cold, but I'm so afraid it is something worse. She has aches and pains with the fever, and she just lies in her bed and doesn't move. Rachel has to feed Freddy while Father tends to Mother.

The influenza is definitely all over the world now. It started across the ocean where the boys are fighting and spread west. It hit the east coast of the United States a few months ago and worked its way out here. Now it's everywhere. There are white cards in windows all over the world. I still just can't really imagine how big it all is. I don't want to think about it. It makes my head ache when I try to think about people all the way in New York, Maine, England and France putting little white cards in their windows. I wonder how many girls my age are thinking about it right now and feeling their heads ache. I wonder how many of those girls will make it through the epidemic. I don't want to think about it anymore.

I went to Palace Beautiful to pray and ask that we might be spared and not have influenza in our home. When I went back downstairs and heard Mother coughing, I knew the answer to my prayer was "no."

I am very afraid!

—Helen

November 8, 1918

Mother is much worse. She coughs so violently, I think she will die. Father is worn out from caring for her. He keeps all of us out of her room so we don't get sick, too.

The Red Cross set up influenza hospitals all around the valley, but Father says they are just places to send the dying and he won't take her. This afternoon I asked if I might fetch Mrs. Phelps to help. Father said no because he didn't want to spread the disease. He alerted the Health Department. They sent a nurse to examine Mother. When she left, she placed a white card in our *front window. Lizzy, Rachel and I cried when we saw it. Anna cried, too, but only because we were crying. She doesn't understand.*

About half an hour after we put out the white card, Mrs. Phelps showed up at our door. I told her she couldn't come in. We were quarantined and it was against the law for anyone to come in or out. She said, "Nonsense!" and marched right in. She told us girls to take off our corsets immediately if we wanted to stay healthy.

Mrs. Phelps opened Mother's bedroom door and I heard her gasp. She closed the door sharply and woke up Freddy.

I wanted to run in and sit with my mother. I wanted to hug her and hold her and make everything normal again. Some people make it through influenza just fine. All the Moodys did. They are all fine. I want Mother to be just fine.

Mrs. Phelps came in and out of the room, completely ignoring us and looking so serious, I couldn't help crying. Lizzy was mad at me for crying even though she was crying herself. Rachel just sat in the rocking chair holding Freddy. The worst was Anna. She stood outside Mother's door knocking softly, saying, "Mother? Mother?"

I can't stand it anymore! I want to run away and have everything be how it was. I want my Palace Beautiful!

—Helen

P.S. It is now nearly midnight. A few hours ago, Mother's coughing stopped. Some men came over with a stretcher. They walked in without knocking and without

even looking at us. They went into Mother's room. When
they came out, they carried her on the stretcher. She was
completely covered with a white sheet. Now I know
everything in the world is over.

The thought of Helen's mother under the white sheet made my stomach roll and churn. I felt like I was going to be sick. I looked at the photo of the Whites and wondered if any of them could have guessed that only a few weeks after that photo was taken, their mother would die. I looked at the photo of my mother. I'd had no idea she was going to die, either. I remember when I found out she wasn't going to come home from the hospital, I felt numb and like someone had kicked me in the head with a hiking boot—dazed, shocked and numb, but aware that something was about to hurt very, very badly.

I thought of Sherrie. This time I would be prepared. I wouldn't be taken off guard. I knew what could happen, and I needed to be ready. Zuzu was so naive, she was actually excited to have the new baby in the house. I can tell her from my own experience that it isn't always a happy time. Sometimes it is the worst time of all.

"Oh my gosh!" said Zuzu when Bella blew out the candle and the thin desolate-hour-gray smoke wrapped its fingers around the small room. "She died! She actually died! Helen's mom died!"

Zuzu jumped up on her knees and crawled to the photo of our mother. She touched it. Her eyes were wide and she looked stunned. Her mouth hung open. Bella rubbed her forehead and closed her eyes.

"I didn't think that was going to happen," said Bella.

"Well, it does!" I said, the anger starting to boil in my stomach. "It happens and it will happen again and again." I managed to swallow my tears, but they sat in a hard lump in my throat that I knew was impossible to hold back forever.

"I'm sorry, Sadie," said Bella.

"It's all right." It wasn't all right, but I was glad she'd said it.

"We've got to finish it!" said Zuzu so loudly that Bella and I both shushed her. "We have to know what happens! The journal is almost over! We have to finish it now! Is Freddy going to die? Is Helen going to die? I have to know!"

Bella picked up the journal and fanned the last pages.

"We only have six more entries. We can wait. We owe it to Helen," said Bella. "I made these." She pulled out about ten red-bird-red crochet squares. "We'll need to make a lot more to finish the shawl. I'm getting fast, though. We can piece the shawl together and wear it when we read the last entries."

I picked up a square. It was soft.

"I can't stay today. I have extra chores to do," said Bella, looking everywhere but at our eyes.

"How come?" said Zuzu.

"Just because," said Bella so softly, she almost didn't say it at all. "I wish I was in this family. You treat me like myself and we have fun. I'm going to be myself at home." She clenched her fists. "I'm going to tell my mom what I think. I want our home to feel like it does here. Before you moved in, I didn't know a family could feel like this. I want to be myself here *and* at home."

We walked Bella out to the front yard. Holly was standing there with her fists on her perfect little hips. Bella must have known she would be there before we even left Palace Beautiful.

"Where have you been, young lady?" said Holly.

Bella didn't answer. She kept her eyes fixed on her thunder-black shoes planted in the pool-green grass.

"Answer me!"

"Here," Bella mumbled.

"Did I give you permission to go out this morning?"

"No."

"Did you deliberately disobey me?"

"Yes." Bella looked up for a moment. "Yes, and I'm glad I did." She looked back down.

"You are grounded, young lady!" Holly stepped across the line that divided the Smiths' yard from the Brookses' yard. Bella followed and they both went inside.

Zuzu and I went up to Palace Beautiful and took a church-white hankie that I got when I was born. We covered the journal and vowed not to read it until Bella came back.

Crackling-Rage Red

THE NEXT MORNING I WENT TO Grandma's house to help her in her yard. She had a beautiful garden and said she needed help tending it. I think maybe she just wanted company. I didn't mind, though.

I came home that afternoon to the sound of Zuzu throwing a tantrum.

"Why do I always have to do all the work?" Zuzu shouted. She was on the living room floor surrounded by a pile of clean laundry—like a little Zuzu island in a sea of cotton polyester. She looked so tiny and overwhelmed that for once, I thought she may actually have a point. It wasn't fair. The job looked ten times bigger than her.

"We all have to do our share," said Dad. I could tell by the little line between his eyebrows that he was overwhelmed, too. Sherrie was resting more and more, but the chores weren't, and there were a lot of them.

"I'll help her," I said, joining Zuzu in the laundry ocean.

"At least someone in this family considers the feelings of children!" she said.

Dad rolled his eyes and went to his room holding a huge mug of water for Sherrie.

"Thanks," Zuzu whispered to me.

"You're welcome."

Zuzu instantly became quiet. She picked up the towels one at a time and folded them neatly. She arranged them in piles according to color—sunset-after-the-rain pink to her right, ancient turquoise to her left and electric limeade at her knees. She had on a little flouncy skirt with checks and stripes. I looked at her knees poking out of the pinky skirt folds. They were scraped and bruised.

"What happened to your knees?" I asked, making a pile of random socks to sort later.

"A kid pushed me down."

"What? What kid pushed you down?" I felt that same panicky feeling as when Sherrie went to the hospital.

"Billy Pratt."

"Why did he push you?"

"He said he wanted my silver dollar and I said no."

"Who's Billy Pratt and how did he know you had a silver dollar?"

"He's Becky Pratt's brother. They live down the street. I was showing the dollar to Becky and he started trying to get it."

I felt the anger bubble and boil in my stomach. Zuzu may be a pest and a drama queen, but she is my sister and no one pushes her to the ground.

"I didn't want to tell Dad or Sherrie," Zuzu continued. "I didn't want to cause trouble. I just came home and cleaned up the scrapes myself."

I was surprised at how grown-up she had been, and a little sad that Zuzu felt she had to go it alone.

"Come here," I said, taking her by the hand and leading her to the window. "Is one of those kids Billy Pratt?"

She pointed to a fat kid with a crew cut who was slapping a smaller kid on the back of the head.

"Come on, we'll finish folding the laundry later."

"What are you gonna do?" asked Zuzu as I practically dragged her out the door and down the street. I didn't answer, because I didn't know what I was going to do. All I knew was that anger was leading me down the street and I wasn't stopping it. When we reached Billy Pratt, the smaller kid was crying.

"Billy Pratt!" I said.

"What do you want?" he said. His eyelids looked heavy, like it took all his strength to hold up his enormous Neanderthal eyebrows.

"You pushed my sister."

"Your sister's a little priss."

"Oh, yeah?" I said. Then it all started to boil over. The crackling-red rage in my stomach burst. It went right to my clenched fists.

He looked at me shaking with rage and started laughing. Between huge belts of laughter, he said, "What're you gonna do, hit me?"

I reeled back and put the force of my entire body into the

strike. My fist rammed into his fat stomach. It sank deeply into the blobby mass and sucked back out. He let out a huge "Ugh" sound and gasped. "What are you doing?" he shouted.

I wasn't finished. I slammed him in the face and he fell onto the sidewalk, his rolls and folds jiggling like Grandma's Jell-O salad. His mouth hung open and his eyes opened even wider.

"Leave my sister alone!" I shouted. I finally caught a glimpse of Zuzu. She stood frozen in the grass with her hands across her mouth and her eyes looking like a cornered rabbit. She looked as shocked and horrified as Billy. I had gone too far.

Suddenly, I was terrified by my own rage. My breath came in fast, trembly snorts, and my body shivered and shook uncontrollably. I had scared myself.

"Come on, Zuzu," I said, forcing the sound to come out of my tight throat.

Billy lay on the concrete with his fist covering his lip and his eyes wide. I took Zuzu's hand and we went home.

As soon as I'd crossed the threshold, I knew I'd made a mistake—a mistake that felt more satisfying than any right choice ever could have felt. But I knew it was only a matter of time before I was really in trouble.

We took our places in the laundry pile. I picked up more socks and looked at my hand. It was bleeding. I felt shocked at my own anger. I hadn't even realized I had that much anger inside, and it scared me to death. I wanted to hold something soft. I dropped the clean socks and stared at the pile, not really seeing it.

"You're gonna get in trouble, you know," Zuzu said, avoiding my eyes.

"I know."

"I think you really hurt him."

"I know."

"Dad is gonna be really mad."

"I know."

She paused for a minute, and then said, "Thanks."

"You're welcome."

Zuzu wrapped her arms around me. She was soft.

"It's going to be all right, Sadie," she said. I felt like crying, but I swallowed it because I am the big sister.

Zuzu released me and we began to fold again. After a minute, I started giggling under my breath. The laughter spilled out of the cracks in my mouth, and Zuzu asked, "What's so funny?"

"Jennifer Meyer's big sister would *never* do that," I said.

"True," she said. Zuzu looked off into space like she was trying to picture Jennifer Meyer's sister belting Billy Pratt. Zuzu snorted, then snorted again, then exploded into a fit of laughter. Then we rolled in the clean laundry, clutching our stomachs and laughing so hard, almost no sound came out of our mouths. Someone knocked at the front door.

"Quick! Go upstairs!" said Zuzu, gulping for air between sobs of laughter. We knew it must be some angry person related to Billy. I also knew that going upstairs wouldn't help, but for some reason, at the time, it seemed like a perfectly logical course of action.

Crackling-Rage Red

"Open this door right now, young lady," said Dad a few minutes later outside my bedroom door.

I did. I stood in front of him bracing myself for what was next.

"What were you thinking?" he said.

"Nothing."

"That's for certain! You should know that the boy almost had to have stitches."

"He pushed Zuzu and hurt her."

"What?"

"He pushed Zuzu down on the ground. She didn't want to bother you or Sherrie, so she cleaned up the cuts herself just before you asked her to fold the laundry."

Dad stood silently for a moment. "Huh," he said, rubbing his chin. "The boy's mother told me he was helping his cousin free a baby bird from the gutter when you attacked him."

I thought of the little kid he was slapping around when we got there and guessed that must have been the cousin he was "helping."

"And you believed her?"

"It did sound strange. . . . He pushed Zuzu down?"

"Yes!"

"Well, tonight, I want you to clean the downstairs bathroom and think about what you did. Violence is never the way to solve problems."

"Yes, Dad."

He continued to look off into space and rub his chin. "So you . . . hit him pretty hard?"

"Yes."

"Huh," Dad said, and walked back down the stairs.

The downstairs bathroom was already immaculate. He knew it and I knew it. I went back down to the living room and helped Zuzu fold the rest of the clothes.

Coffin Black

I DIDN'T REALIZE HOW HARD IT would be to wait to read the journal—and not even peek. The next day, I found myself walking up to Palace Beautiful again and again, but not going inside. I thought about Helen. I thought about influenza. I thought about the singing Zuzu heard in the attic, and I couldn't wait any longer. I just had to know what had happened to Helen. After dinner, I went up the attic stairs. I opened the door and jumped so violently, I nearly fell over.

"Zuzu!" I said in a kind of shout-whisper. "What are you doing here?"

"Nothing," she said. "What are you doing here?"

"Nothing . . . too."

We stood silently, waiting for the other to confess.

"Fine!" Zuzu said, throwing her arms in the air. "I was going to have a little teeny peek at the journal. Go ahead, lecture me."

"I was going to have a peek, too."

"You were?"

"Yes."

"Sadie! How could you?"

"What!? You were going to, too!"

"Don't change the subject!"

"I . . ." Just then, we heard a tapping sound. Zuzu and I turned to the sound. We looked out the east window and saw Bella in her attic tossing pebbles out her window to get our attention. The pebbles tapped the glass and then fell to the yard below. We went to the window and opened it.

"Here," said Bella, tossing something bigger than the pebble from her window to ours. "I gotta go." She closed the window and turned out her attic light.

Zuzu picked up the little bundle. It was a bunch of redbird-red crochet squares with a coffin-black ribbon tied around it.

Zuzu took the squares to Palace Beautiful and I followed. She laid them in the journal's box.

"We better go before we get too tempted and accidentally start reading," said Zuzu.

"Yeah."

Just as we were about to crawl out of the little room, we heard the attic door creak open. Zuzu and I froze. I heard footsteps walk across the threshold. They were Dad's. I could tell by the clomping of his shoes. He started to hum and we heard boxes shuffling.

"He doesn't know we're here," mouthed Zuzu.

"Shhhh!" I mouthed back.

The humming stopped. The footsteps stopped. We held our breath, puffing out our cheeks and covering our mouths in case any breath escaped and we would be discovered.

It seemed like we stayed that way for hours. It was probably only seconds, but our cheeks turned bang-smash red from lack of oxygen. The humming started again and we knew if we just stayed quiet for another few seconds, we would be safe.

I heard Dad's shoes clomp to the attic door. It creaked behind him and clicked shut.

"Whoa!" said Zuzu, still mouthing the words. "That was close!"

When we were sure he was downstairs again, we crept out of the little room and left the attic.

Dried-Up Beige

THE NEXT MORNING I DECIDED TO take my watercolors to the front yard and paint a picture of the sycamore tree. When I opened the front door, I found a bigger bundle of red-bird-red crochet squares lying on the porch. Calamity, who followed me like a shadow, stood at my feet batting and picking at the soft squares. I took the bundle inside and placed them in Palace Beautiful. Then I went back out and sat down in the cool grass of the front yard.

I mixed colors to get dried-up beige, fresh-air green and warm-cookies brown. I painted so-very-very-deep blue behind the tree and the almost-white blue of the mountains. It felt so calming to be sitting in the warm sun painting a picture of the tree—the tree the Whites had planted. I smelled the air and wondered if that was what it smelled like when Anna and Rachel were tending the tree and playing in this very yard. I thought of their father wrapping the tree against the cold and saying it would someday be big enough to tap on the glass of

Helen's window. I wondered when Bella would be ungrounded so we could finish the journal. I wondered if Sherrie would have to rest all the time until the baby came. I began to think that sometimes there's just nothing a person can do about a situation, so they sit in the grass and wonder.

I couldn't do anything about Sherrie, Helen or Bella. All I could do was watch the sycamore tree bend and sway in the summer breeze and think.

"That was it," said Zuzu, sitting down beside me just as I had put the final brushstroke on the picture.

"What?" I looked at Zuzu. She looked like she did in the laundry pile, like she had learned something about life that wasn't good, but just had to accept it as a fact.

"You were humming."

"What are you talking about?"

"Just now, you were humming a little song. That is what I heard in the attic the other day. It was you." She looked at the grass and picked a handful. Her pretty lips fell into a pretty frown.

"I didn't even know I was humming. What was the song?"

Zuzu hummed a few notes.

"That was the song Mom used to sing to me."

"I remember it. I wonder if she sang it to me before she died."

"I used to sing it to you."

"Thank you, Sadie," she said, and she kissed my cheek. We sat silently for a long time watching the fat white clouds climb across the sky.

Before I went to bed that night, I found five more crochet squares sitting on the front porch.

I untied the black ribbon and dangled an end for Calamity, who grabbed it and chewed it with her tiny teeth. Then I took the ribbon, Calamity and the squares to Palace Beautiful. Zuzu was there.

"Not trying to peek again!?" I said.

She didn't say anything. She just shook her head.

"What are you doing here, then?" I asked, sitting down beside her. She reached up and touched the picture of our mother.

"I . . . I don't know who she is," she said. "I don't remember anything about her. I never really had a mom until Sherrie, and now she's going to have a baby that's really hers—not like me."

I had never thought about the fact that Zuzu had never known our mother. I knew it in my head, of course, but I had never thought of what that meant to her life. Calamity crawled out of my lap and curled up in Zuzu's.

"Sometimes I just want to yell and scream," said Zuzu.

"You always yell and scream."

"Sadie!"

"Sorry."

"I don't want to get left behind again. Sometimes, I just need to yell and scream and I can't help it."

"No one is going to leave you, Zuzu."

"Mom did. Grandma Brooks said she is up in heaven with all the other people who love her and she's happy, but what about me? Does it count that I never had a real mom?

Does she care about that when she's sitting up there in heaven enjoying everyone? Does she care that I grew up without her?"

Calamity purred and nudged Zuzu's ear. I didn't know what to say. I didn't have any answers, and that made me sadder than I'd ever felt before.

Anti-Color White

WHEN I WENT DOWNSTAIRS FOR breakfast, Sherrie was scrubbing the kitchen floor on her hands and knees.

"What are you doing?" I asked.

"I just felt like cleaning, I guess."

I looked around the dining room, then the kitchen. There was not a speck of dust or a crumb on anything to be seen anywhere. "What time did you get up?"

"The early bird gets the worm," she said, wiping a stray strand of hair from her eyes.

"What are you doing?" said Zuzu, coming up behind me.

"She's cleaning," I said.

"Oh." Zuzu went into the kitchen and poured a bowl of Frosty Cocoa Flakes.

I sat down on the floor by Sherrie, who scrubbed so furiously, she didn't seem to notice I was there until I said, "Does Dad know you're doing this?"

"I have a right to clean my own house," she said.

"In other words, no."

She stopped and mopped her forehead with her sleeve. She turned to look at me, dropping her scrub brush into the bucket of cleaning water.

"I declare, Sadie, you grew in your sleep! You look practically grown and more and more like Jackie O. every day."

"Have I grown, Sherrie?" asked Zuzu. "Do I look more like Jackie O?"

"Of course," she answered, retrieving her scrub brush and not even looking at Zuzu. Zuzu smiled and strutted proudly back to the kitchen.

The next day, Sherrie was cleaning again. She was unstoppable, and even Dad couldn't talk her out of it. She insisted that she felt fine and that if she had to spend another minute in bed, she'd go crazy. She hardly ate or drank. She just scrubbed, polished, wiped, sanitized and dusted just about everything in the house.

Zuzu and I tried to help, but for some reason, Sherrie wanted to do it all herself and sent us out to play. I don't think she had ever sent us away before—even to the front yard. At least she let us eat breakfast first.

Zuzu and I sat at the table by ourselves. Sherrie was in the parlor, probably cleaning the paint right off the wall.

Zuzu was quiet. She stared at the cereal on her spoon like she was looking right through it. "Do you think . . . do you think Freddy will die?"

"I don't know," I said.

"What about . . . never mind," she said.

"What about what?"

"What about Sherrie?"

I turned and faced the wall. My stomach knotted and I felt a sharp pain behind my eye. I didn't want to talk about it.

"No," I said.

"Sorry, Sadie."

I didn't say anything, and I didn't feel like saying anything for the rest of the day. I couldn't stop following Sherrie around. I tried to think of reasons to be with her constantly, but I knew the real reason—fear. I couldn't lose her like I had my mother. Sherrie moved so slowly and rested so often, I knew it would be time soon, but I wished it was forever away.

Later that day, as Zuzu and I went to the kitchen to help get lunch ready, Sherrie said, "I'm going to clean that attic this afternoon, top to bottom, ceiling to floor."

Zuzu and I looked at each other. Palace Beautiful was hidden enough that anyone just in the attic to get something or put something away and leave would most likely miss it, but if Sherrie tried to clean up there as earnestly as she had the rest of the house, she'd surely find it.

"No!" said Zuzu, dropping her spoon on the floor and knocking over her glass of milk.

"Zuzu," Sherrie said, annoyed. "I just scrubbed that floor."

"Wait," Zuzu whispered to herself. Then she turned to me and whispered, "I'll take care of this."

A few minutes later, Sherrie filled up the scrubbing bucket and started up the stairs. Just as she was about to reach the attic steps, Zuzu began to wail, "Sherrie! Sadie took my new jelly shoes and threw them in the mud!"

"I did not!" I said.

"She did, Sherrie, and now I can't find one of them! Life is so unfair!" Then she turned to me and whispered, "Play along."

I all of a sudden got what was going on. Zuzu was throwing a fake tantrum to distract Sherrie from going into the attic.

"Oh," I said. "Um, you started it!" I yelled. I'm sure it sounded fake because Zuzu turned and shot me a mean look. "I mean! No, I didn't!"

Zuzu nodded. "No one in Jennifer Meyer's family would ever throw perfectly lovely jelly shoes in the mud! They respect the property of a little girl! They don't cast her beautiful things aside! They love her!"

The tantrum went on and on until Zuzu was sure Sherrie had forgotten about the attic and had to lie down for a nap. The scene was repeated three more times until Sherrie gave up the idea of cleaning the attic altogether. I have to admit, it was pretty brilliant. I suppose, in this case, being from the cabbage patch was a very good thing.

That night, I went up to Palace Beautiful just to be alone for a while.

I turned on the camping lantern and lay down on the quilt. I tried to picture what the house looked like when Helen lived there. I tried to imagine what it would feel like to have the city shut down and friends dying all around. The thought made my head ache, and I thought of Sherrie and the baby.

People think that women don't die in childbirth anymore, but they do.

Sherrie and Dad had picked out a crib for the nursery, and Dad had gone to pick it up. All of a sudden, I realized I was going to have an actual new sibling—a little Anna or Freddy. I guess I'd already known it in my head, but for some reason, I suddenly understood it in my soul. I didn't know what to think. I didn't know if I liked the idea or not.

I wondered what it felt like for Helen to lose her mother. I knew what it felt like for me. I felt sick to my stomach.

Dad arrived home a few minutes later with the anti-color-white crib. I left Palace Beautiful to have a look.

Dad, Zuzu and I were standing in the nursery admiring the crib parts that would have to be assembled when Sherrie walked in. She looked tired, but she was still smiling. She always smiled—even when she knew that very soon, everything could be over.

Bubbly-Churning Green

THE NEXT MORNING STARTED OUT fine. After breakfast, I stood on the front step and stretched. Something about the air felt different. Calamity purred against my ankles. I picked her up and rubbed her soft side against my cheek. Suddenly, she meowed and scratched my face. Instinctively, I nearly dropped her. I caught myself just in time. I set her gently on the step, and she continued to purr and play with my toes. I felt my cheek. It was bleeding.

I looked back at the sky. The sun was just peeking out from behind the mountains. In Salt Lake City, sunrise takes a long time. Since it rises in the east, it has to climb to the top of the mountains before we can see it. The sun shines in the western parts of the valley long before it hits the homes in the eastern part of the valley. In the morning in our neighborhood, it's like sitting in the shade of a tree—it's not dark night, but it's not quite sunny either.

I breathed in the air and realized what was different. It was totally still. The canyons usually sigh out the cold night air in the morning. But today, nothing moved, except Calamity at my feet. The stillness felt odd and unnatural. Fine strands of barely visible clouds hung motionless in the sky.

Bella was supposed to be ungrounded today, but she hadn't shown up. I wondered if she was grounded all over again. Her house was dark—darker than usual.

Zuzu and I helped Dad set up the nursery. Sherrie wanted it decorated in whispery yellows and greens so the baby could enjoy it whether it was a boy or a girl.

Dad set up the crib and brought in the rocking chair that used to belong to my mom. It was an antique that belonged to my mother's mother. Sherrie wanted to keep it instead of getting a new one because she says they don't make things like they used to. I imagined my mother used to sit with me in that chair like Rachel rocking little Freddy.

Zuzu and I put up the curtains and put sheets and blankets on the little crib mattress. We didn't talk as we worked— Zuzu because she was so immersed in the task, and Dad and I because we knew from experience what all of this could mean. Sherrie slept the entire morning. I hoped she didn't have any dreams.

A few hours later, I sat on the living room floor folding clothes when Zuzu came bursting into the room.

"Sadie, come quick!"

"What is it?" I said, jumping off the bed automatically and following Zuzu. She ran to the front window and pointed with her whole arm.

"That! They've been out there talking forever," said Zuzu.

Bella was standing in her front lawn with Jason Prince. They stood facing each other. Jason was tall. I hadn't realized it before. He leaned down, gave her a quick kiss on the cheek and ran away. The kiss was so quick, I wasn't sure it even had time to reach her cheek. She blushed so deeply, I could see it from my living room window.

"Zuzu, why are we watching this?" I said, stepping away from the window.

"I don't know," she said, staring like she was in some kind of trance. I reached over and pulled the curtains shut.

Ten minutes later, Bella came over. Her face was flushed and rosy. Zuzu and I pretended we hadn't seen anything. Bella picked up Calamity and rubbed her feather-ash fur against her cheeks.

"She is so soft," Bella cooed. "Just like a kiss."

Zuzu rolled her eyes and took Calamity from Bella. She rubbed the kitten against her own cheek.

"She is so soft," said Zuzu. "Just like a cat." She said it in a decidedly smug tone and handed the kitten back.

"I love cats," said Bella, looking far, far away. Zuzu and I looked at each other and couldn't help giggling a little. Bella didn't notice.

Someone knocked at the front door. Sherrie and Dad came out of their room. Sherrie walked slowly, and it looked like a lot of work. Zuzu beat her and Dad to the door.

"Sorry to bother you all, but is Kristin here?" Holly asked, standing on the front step in her apron. The apron covered a spotless dress that was small in the middle and opened wide at the bottom like the letter A. I wondered why she might need an apron when she never got a spot on anything. Maybe it was some kind of magazine-ad-mom uniform.

"Yes, come in," said Sherrie.

"Kristin, come home right now. We talked about this."

"No." Bella put her hands on her hips and raised her chin parallel to the floor, unlike its usual position when her mom was around—pointing to her chest.

"What did you say?" Holly looked astonished and had to compose herself for a moment before she could fully return to her magazine-ad-mom state.

"I said, no."

"Kristin!" Holly's eyes widened, and she stared at Bella like everything else in the room had disappeared except for her daughter.

"It's Belladonna Desolation!"

"It's Kristin Anne Smith." Holly turned to the rest of us. "She says these silly things sometimes."

"No!" said Bella. "Kristin Anne is the girl you wanted. She doesn't exist, but I do!" Bella's arms fell to her sides, but her chin stayed up.

"She's always been difficult," Holly said, turning to Sherrie for sympathy. Sherrie just crossed her arms almost like she was from the cabbage patch.

"By difficult do you mean I'm not willing to pretend to be the daughter you wanted?"

"Don't be ridiculous, Kristin. Come home right now. I don't know what you're talking about." Holly spoke with a desperation that made the last bits of the magazine-ad-mom look disappear completely.

"You do know what I'm talking about," Bella insisted.

"Kristin Smith! How dare you make me look foolish in front of the neighbors!" Holly looked like someone had just proved that the world was actually flat and she had to re-arrange her entire belief system while standing in our front room.

"I'm not making you look foolish, Mom, you're doing it to yourself. The Brooks family is nice to me and likes me to be here. I like being at their house. It feels happy. Our house doesn't. It feels empty and black."

"Kristin, you are taking crazy. You're just a kid. You don't know what you're talking about. You're just tired."

"I *do* know what I'm talking about. I want to be myself and not get punished for talking to my friends or coming over to play."

Holly stood silently. "I . . . ," she started, and then she trailed off.

"I love you, Mom, but you have to realize I'm a person. I just want to feel happy at home like I feel here. I'm not ask-ing you to be a different kind of mom, or person or anything, I just want you to be happy to have me around."

"I . . . okay," said Holly. Her voice trembled. Her eyes were huge, and she looked like someone had just slapped her across the face and said, "Snap out of it!"

"Okay, you can stay," she said half in a daze. She turned around and walked out the door.

We all stood silent for a moment, trying to take in what had just happened.

Bella was shaking and I couldn't say anything. Dad and

Sherrie didn't say anything either, but as we started to go up to Palace Beautiful, I could have sworn I heard Sherrie whisper, "Way to go!"

"Wow!" said Zuzu when we were all sitting in Palace Beautiful. "Do you think your mom will listen?"

"I don't know. But either way, I am going to speak up more. Look at my hands." Bella held out her palms. They were shaking. She laughed, and then hugged Zuzu and me.

"What do you think will happen when you get home?" I asked.

"I don't know, but I do know it will be better than before, because I know I can say what I need to say—even if she doesn't listen."

Bella took two more bundles of red squares from her skirt pockets. Zuzu had the one that she was willing to make, and I had the small bundle I'd made while Bella was grounded.

"These are the last squares," said Bella. "Let's piece the shawl together before we read."

The three of us sat sewing and talking until, at last, we had a shawl. I held it up to the light and we all smiled.

"Helen would be proud," said Zuzu.

I laid the shawl across Zuzu's shoulders and handed her the journal. Bella lit the candle and Zuzu began to read the last entries.

November 9, 1918

I can't seem to think. I feel like everything is a dream and I just can't figure it out. Mrs. Phelps stayed the night with us because now Father is coughing. A few minutes ago, Lizzy went back to bed. I felt her head and she is burning.

Father is very ill and so is Lizzy. Mrs. Phelps is tired and I'm sure her family needs her, but she still stays and helps.

Father's fever is very high, but he doesn't cough like Mother did. Mrs. Phelps taught Rachel and me to rotate his body every few minutes to help his lungs. We turn him on one side and then the other, but never on his back or stomach. Mrs. Phelps made him a special tea and it seems to help some. She told us to keep all the fireplaces burning to warm up the house and draw out the sickness. Rachel and I take turns bringing in the wood and stoking the fires.

Lizzy isn't as bad as Father. She can still communicate some. She has the fever, and she coughs, but not anything like Father or Mother.

Rachel and I tend Anna and Freddy. Freddy is restless and fussy. We have to teach him to use a bottle, but he doesn't want to. He and Anna spent a good deal of the day crying. Anna cannot understand where Mother is. We try to explain it to her, but she still calls for her day and night. She says she just wants to be with Mother. Rachel and I pray that she won't. We are getting very tired.

Something has happened to me. I can't feel. My brain is cloudy and muddled, and it's like I'm not awake. I feel a dull ache in my soul, but nothing else—not sad, happy,

angry, scared or anything. I just take care of Anna and
Freddy. It feels as if part of me has turned to granite like
the mountains.

—Helen

November 11, 1918

Father and Lizzy are making slight improvements
today, but they are both very, very ill. Mrs. Phelps is
tired, and I am afraid she will have to leave soon.

When I woke up this morning, I heard shouting in the
street. I looked out and saw people dancing. I put up my
window to hear what was going on. They were dancing
because today, the war ended.

I put my window back down and wrapped Anna in my
red shawl. She has not left my side since they took Mother
away. She follows me to stoke the fires. She follows me to
cook, she follows me to do the washing and last night she
slept in my bed. She clung to the shawl like it was
Mother. She put her thumb in her mouth and laid her
head in my lap.

I looked back at the people dancing in the street and
thought I should be happy, but I can't feel. I couldn't go
outside because of our white card, so I just looked out the
window and stroked Anna's hair.

I stirred the fire and added some more wood and Anna
began coughing.

Mrs. Phelps taught Rachel and me how do everything
to care for Father and Lizzy. We know how to turn them,
how to make their special tea, how to rub Vicks on their

chests to keep their fevers down, and how to keep them restful and as comfortable as we can. She saw to it that we had enough wood in the house to keep the fires going. At dinnertime, she packed up and went home. She looked so exhausted, I was worried for her. I was more worried for Rachel and me though. Freddy will only take a bottle from Rachel now, and Anna needs so much attention. After Mrs. Phelps left, Rachel and I knelt down and prayed like we had never prayed before.

When I put Anna down this evening, she felt warm. She coughed a few times, and I had to plug my ears. I can't stand the thought of her being ill, too. What are Rachel and I going to do?

—Helen

Zuzu handed the journal to Bella and placed the shawl around her shoulders. Bella read:

November 12, 1918

All night Anna was burning and listless. She whimpered and called for Mother. I turned her, made her tea, rubbed Vicks on her chest, and tried to keep her comfortable, but she was dead before the sun finished rising.

I placed her doll Millie in her arms and covered Anna's little body with my red shawl. She is with Mother now, just like she wanted. I didn't know who to call about taking her body away, so I sat on her bed and held her hand until the fire in her fireplace burned out and her little

hand turned cold. Then I walked out and closed her
bedroom door. I couldn't think. I couldn't feel.

Father and Lizzy's fevers persist and Freddy is fretful.
Rachel and I are beyond exhausted.

By this evening Rachel was feverish and coughing. I
sent her to bed and took Freddy on my lap. I looked in
his little eyes and he smiled at me. It was more than I
could bear. Some of the stone in my heart cracked and
I wept like I was a baby myself.

Now Freddy is sleeping and I hear coughing from all
over the house. I'm in my Palace Beautiful. It's dark
except for my little candle and I'm alone. I need to stoke
the fires and make the tea. I'm so tired!

—Helen

November 13, 1918

Before Freddy woke this morning, I took the photo of
our family and pinned it up in my Palace Beautiful. Then
I went through Mother's jewelry box and found the
necklace Father gave her when they were courting. I hung
it on the nail that held the photo. I lay under the quilt and
looked at the photograph and tried to make it real. Even
in the attic, I heard the coughing. I'm beginning to love
the sound. Anna's room is so still and silent.

Rachel is ill now. It is only Freddy and I who are
well. Father and Lizzy make very little improvement each
day. They get no worse, but no better. Rachel is now
burning with fever and crying all the time with the aches.
Freddy cries, too. I try to get him to take a bottle, but he

won't have it. I rock him and he won't be calm. I walk
with him and carry him into the sick rooms to care for
everyone. He is very tired and so am I. I haven't slept the
night through in days.

The white card sits motionless in our front window,
and I just work without thinking. It is too hard to think
and even harder to feel, so I just tend to everyone and try
to hold my exhausted body together. The white card sits
in the Phelpses' window now, too, so I know Mrs. Phelps
is not coming back to help. It is just Freddy and me.
Father, Lizzy and Rachel shiver and burn in their beds
while Anna lies silent and cold upstairs. I don't even
know where they've taken Mother. I am exhausted. I
wonder if this is all real.

—Helen

Bella handed the journal to me and placed the red-bird-red
shawl around my shoulders. We didn't say a word. The little
room was completely still. I began to read.

November 14, 1918
Freddy refuses to drink a bottle for me. He screams
and wails and I carry him into the sick rooms and tend to
Father, Lizzy and Rachel as best I can.

In moments of quiet, I take him up to my Palace
Beautiful to rest. He cries no tears now, and he is hoarse
from the shrieking. He is so hungry, he is beginning to
waste. I just hold him close and try to calm him.

Father and Lizzy are the same as they have been.

Rachel is much worse. I turn her and make her tea, keep her fire going, but she hardly even responds to my presence. Her fever is so high, her eyes roll around in her head and her mouth hangs open like she is trying to speak, but nothing comes out.

I am in my Palace Beautiful and Freddy is by my side sleeping. He cries less here, and I think we will sleep here until he can be comforted in any other way. I hate to sleep. I don't want tomorrow to come.

—Helen

November 15, 1918

Little Freddy drank from his bottle for me today. This morning, I took him in my arms and rocked him in Mother's chair. I sang to him, and he watched my face intently. I felt his little, warm body relax softly into my arms, and I knew I loved him. I warmed a bottle and this time he drank. He drank furiously, and then he fell asleep still in my arms.

He may have needed me to care for him, but at the moment, I needed nothing more than the soft warm bundle against my chest. I fell asleep, too, for a few minutes until Rachel needed me. I'm so very tired.

Freddy and I are in my Palace Beautiful right now. I don't want to leave him. We will both sleep here tonight. I feel so tired and cold. I'm sure if I rest a while, I will warm up and feel better. I'm so worn out that my body is sore like I just fell down a flight of steps. I can't stop shaking. I just need a little rest. I am too tired to tend the *fires all night again. I got blankets to wrap Freddy and me up with in Palace Beautiful so he and I can keep warm. It's all I can do. I am so tired.*

Once Father said that a man's home is his Palace Beautiful, that the world can knock all it wants, but unless we open the door, it can't come in. Well, it did come in. Now I'm afraid for little Freddy. The house is no longer safe, and even my little Palace Beautiful here in the attic grows cold. For Freddy, my arms are the only Palace Beautiful left. I hope they are good enough.

—Helen

"That's it," I said, closing the book. I held it in my arms and felt the red-bird-red shawl around my shoulders. Even though it was the middle of summer, I couldn't help shivering.

"Helen," whispered Bella, and she blew out the candle.

"That's all?" said Zuzu. "That can't be all!" Her lip quivered, and then she threw her head back and burst into tears. She wailed and howled like the Great Dog.

"That can't be all! That can't be all!" repeated Bella.

"Well, it is!" I shouted. Suddenly I felt the writhing-red anger swelling in my stomach again. "It is the end! Sometimes there isn't a happy ending! Sometimes everything falls apart and that's the end! Sometimes the end is the worst end in the world!" I burst into tears and couldn't stop myself. Zuzu sniffed and stopped crying. She put her arms around me, and Bella followed. Their arms felt warm and I stopped shaking, but I couldn't stop crying. I knew too well that sometimes things fall apart and never go back to the way they are supposed to be.

"It's going to be all right, Sadie," said Bella in a tone so warm and confident that I almost believed her.

I sat in Bella's and Zuzu's arms with Calamity nipping at my toes until I stopped crying. I was so glad to have my little sister and my friend with me in Palace Beautiful. I thought of Helen alone here and sick with Freddy. I may have lost my mom, but the truth was, sitting here in our little secret room, I hadn't lost everything.

Suddenly we heard a loud tapping sound. We all looked at one another.

"Who's there?" mouthed Bella to Zuzu and me. We both shrugged. The tapping grew louder and we grew quieter. Calamity stretched her paws and yawned. She padded out the doorway before we could stop her. It was too late. Whoever was out there would see Calamity and know we were there.

We waited for someone to peek around the curtain. We kept waiting. Calamity mewed and batted the curtain from the outside. We still heard the tapping, but no one looked in. We sat perfectly still, trying not to breathe.

After a few minutes, I realized I knew the sound. It wasn't a person. It was the sycamore tapping the window like it does in my room. I'd never heard it tap the attic window before.

"It's all right, it's the tree," I said. Bella and Zuzu exhaled like they had been holding their breath the whole time. We all climbed out and looked out the south window. The tree was tossing and whipping around like the tree in the orchard that lost its apples.

The sky was half light and half dark. The sun still shone

over the mountains, but from the west, fat black clouds rolled and tumbled over each other just overhead.

"We were in there only a little while," said Zuzu. "It was just sunny."

"It's not anymore," I said. "Bella, you better go home before the storm hits."

Bella nodded, and we followed her down the stairs and outside to the front step. Bella ran to her house with the wind pulling and tugging at her all-is-lost-black skirt.

When a person grows up in Texas, they are used to storms. I remember many times the sky turning bubbly-churning green and the words *tornado warning* running across the bottom of the TV screen. This was exactly what tornado weather felt like.

Zuzu and I stood on the front steps looking up at the sky.

"There aren't any tornadoes in Utah, right?" Zuzu asked.

"I don't know," I said. The wind came up the front walk and smacked us so hard, we bolted for the door. Inside it felt quiet and still.

"Whoa!" said Dad, walking to the front window. "Where did that come from? It was sunny just a few minutes ago." He went back to the kitchen to work on dinner.

Zuzu and I watched at the window. We saw other faces peering out at the storm from neighbors' homes all up and down the street. That's one difference between people from Texas and people from Utah. People from Texas say, "Huh, it's gonna storm," and then they get on with whatever they were doing. People from Utah press their noses against the glass, look up at the clouds and watch. They aren't used to it like we are. This time, Zuzu and I decided to join our Utah neighbors and watch.

Clouds filled in the last of the sky's clear spaces. The wind thrashed at the trees and bushes.

Zuzu waved at Mrs. Carter, who sat at her front window across the street watching the clouds. She didn't see us or wave back. Then I realized that it wasn't just the Carters' house, it used to be Martha and Paul Phelps' house. I suddenly felt like I was watching Mrs. Phelps at her front window.

Lightning lit up the street. A few seconds later, thunder tumbled down it. It started to rain. It fell in sparse fat drops for a minute or two, then dumped to the ground in blur-white sheets.

We heard thunder. We heard the rain pummeling the ground. We heard the wind tearing through the sycamore, and then we heard the worst sound of all.

"Norman!" screamed Sherrie from the bedroom.

Dad bolted from the kitchen into their room, almost flying. He came out just as fast. "Girls! I'm taking Sherrie to the hospital right now! Sadie, call Grandma Brooks to come over."

"I will," I said, running for the phone in a blind panic.

Dad helped Sherrie out of their room and out the front door so fast, we didn't even get to say good-bye. He helped her into the car and they drove away just as I got Grandma's answering machine.

"She's not home, Zuzu," I said. "We'll just have to take

care of ourselves until she gets back." Just then we heard a crash from upstairs.

Zuzu and I ran up. I opened my bedroom door and Calamity darted out of the room. The sycamore had smashed right through my window, and the storm roared around my bedroom destroying everything in its path. I ran in. Everything was wrong.

Under the window, broken glass lay in jagged sheets and sparkly splinters. I started grabbing the biggest pieces.

"What are you doing?" shouted Zuzu, still in the doorway.

"Putting it back together! It's all broken. Everything's broken!"

"Sadie, get out of there!"

"I can't! I have to put it together again!" I felt a sharp corner of glass slice into my fingers. I couldn't stop. I knew I must be bleeding, but all I could see was broken glass all over the floor.

"Get out, Sadie!" yelled Zuzu, running in and grabbing my arm. She pulled me out of the room and picked up Calamity, who shivered in a hallway corner. Zuzu took Calamity and me upstairs to Palace Beautiful to wait out the storm.

My hands were shivering and numb. They were bleeding from the broken glass. Zuzu picked out the tiny splinters and wrapped my hands in one of Sherrie's good towels. The tree tapped at the attic window, but the glass didn't break.

Spun-Gold Yellow

"HELLO? HELLO?" CALLED A VOICE FROM downstairs. The storm had stopped and everything was quiet. Zuzu, Calamity and I left the attic and found Grandma Brooks standing in our parlor.

"Where were you girls?" She looked worried.

"We tried to call," I said.

"Well, I got a call from your dad at the hospital. You get to stay with me tonight."

"How's Sherrie?" asked Zuzu.

"Well, the baby is pretty determined to be born as soon as possible even though it's not supposed to be here for a few more weeks. The doctors want to wait as long as they can, and Sherrie is in the middle of the fight."

"Is she . . . is she okay?" I asked.

"The doctors are doing the best they can to keep her comfortable."

"But is she okay?" I felt panic rising in my throat and a numbness in my limbs.

"Oh, honey, I'm sure she's going to be fine," said Grandma. I didn't believe her. Zuzu started to cry. I couldn't. I just stood there frozen.

"Come on out here and have a look." Grandma Brooks opened the front door and motioned for us to step outside.

It looked like the end of the world. Well, maybe not that bad, but almost. Two huge boughs of the sycamore lay torn on the ground. A few trees in neighbors' yards lay on their sides, their muddy roots pointing unnaturally at the spun-gold-yellow sky. The street was covered in leaves, branches and gritty volcanic-black roof shingles.

"Whoa!" said Zuzu. She tugged on Grandma's sweater and pointed to my bedroom window.

"Oh, my goodness!" she exclaimed. "I better call someone to look at that."

A few minutes later, Zuzu and I packed our backpacks and walked to Grandma Brooks' house. I carried Calamity in the little box she used as a bed. She seemed comfortable and content, like nothing had happened. I thought of Sherrie in the hospital. I thought of the storm ripping through my room. I thought of spending the night away from my own bed and felt like the trees lying in the street on their sides—tossed, torn and uprooted.

"Sadie," whispered Zuzu, tugging softly at the covers. We shared a bed in the guest room at Grandma's house. "Sadie, are you awake?"

"Yeah."

It was dark. Much darker than usual, since the storm had broken the streetlight in front of the house. It didn't feel like Grandma Brooks' house when it was so dark.

"I brought it," said Zuzu.

"Brought what?"

"The journal. I brought it in my backpack."

For some reason, the fact that the journal was in the room with us made things feel a little better. It made the dark little room feel like Palace Beautiful.

"Thanks, Zuzu."

"You're welcome."

I leaned over and kissed her cheek.

Pillow-Feather Blue

I WOKE UP SORE FROM ZUZU'S constant kicking and the cuts on my hand.

I smelled bacon and heard thunder. Calamity climbed up on my head and licked my ear. It tickled. I took the kitten in my arms and felt her purr. I needed her softness.

Sharp ticks and tacks, like handfuls of glass beads, were hitting the window. It was hailing.

Zuzu woke up and rubbed her eyes. "Jennifer Meyer has two guest beds in their spare room," she groaned.

Zuzu, Calamity and I went downstairs. Grandma stood at the stove flipping a couple of fried eggs.

"Good morning, sleepyheads," she said. "Have a seat." She motioned to the table, which was covered with food. Even breakfast at Grandma's was a feast. There was a pan of cinnamon rolls, the kind that pop out of a can. There was bacon, sausage, hash browns and toast with blackberry jam.

There was orange juice in tiny plastic Tupperware cups and milk in a glass pitcher in case we were still thirsty.

I started loading a plate and Zuzu did the same. I wasn't hungry, though, and I was pretty sure Zuzu wasn't either.

"Any . . . any word?" I asked.

Grandma Brooks shook her head and smiled. "These things can take time," she said. "Your dad called earlier to let us know that nothing has happened yet and it looks like it might be a while."

Just then, the phone rang and we all jumped. Grandma walked calmly to the phone. Zuzu and I dropped our forks and looked at each other.

"Hello?" she said in a tone of voice that told me she was as anxious as I was. I tried to hear, but the phone was on the other side of the kitchen wall. Zuzu and I jumped up and put our ears against the wall. I wanted to hear, but at the same time, I didn't.

"Oh, hi, Roberta," said Grandma Brooks.

"Roberta?" said Zuzu.

"Maybe it's a nurse or something," I said.

"Yes. . . . I suppose so. . . . Yes . . . yes," said Grandma. "Well, tell Dolly I can't get the potatoes to her this morning, but if she wants, I can do it next week instead."

"It's just her friend," I said to Zuzu, and we went back to the kitchen table. My heart was still beating fast, but I sank down into my chair half from fear of still not knowing and half from relief that instead of being about Sherrie being in trouble it was just about potatoes.

I took a piece of toast from the pile that seemed awfully high for the three of us.

The doorbell rang. It was Bella.

"Is everything all right?" she said, shaking the rain out of her black skirt. She had on a Black Morrisons T-shirt. The four guys were wearing heavy eye makeup and lipstick outside the lines. It looked like Zuzu getting overly enthusiastic with a red Popsicle. They were standing around a gravestone that said "Death to Mediocrity."

"I went to your house and no one was home. I thought you might be here," she said, walking in like it was her own house.

"Sherrie's in the hospital," said Zuzu.

Bella's face lit up. "Did she have the baby?" she asked.

I was surprised by the happy reaction. It was the last reaction I could imagine having at the moment. "We don't know yet," I said.

Bella walked past me into the kitchen. Grandma Brooks hung up the phone, and Bella handed her a small package wrapped in newspaper.

"What's this?" Grandma asked. "For me?"

Bella nodded. Grandma opened the package and pulled out two shine-white crocheted dishrags.

"I made them myself . . . for you." Bella smiled and so did Grandma.

"My, these are fine!" she said, and Bella beamed brighter. "Thank you so much!"

"This is for you," Bella said, handing me a piece of paper.

I opened it. "It looks like an address."

"It is. Sally Kimball's daughter called this morning."

"What?" I said. "What did she say?"

"She said she found this on an old letter. It's Helen's address. At least it used to be."

"What?!" Zuzu and I cried in unison.

"Helen White?" said Zuzu, grabbing the paper out of my hand.

"Helen Phelps—she married Paul!" Bella grinned.

"She did not!" squealed Zuzu.

"She did!"

I asked Grandma if she could take us to the address. It was on the other side of town—too far to walk, and besides, it was raining.

"What's going on, girls?" asked Grandma, wiping her hands on her apron.

Zuzu dashed upstairs and came down holding the journal.

"This," Zuzu said, handing it to her. "It belonged to a Helen White who used to live in our house. We found it in the attic."

Grandma Brooks looked through the pages. "My, this is a treasure. I'm sure anyone would be glad to have this back after all these years," she said. She handed it back to Zuzu.

"We've been trying to find her for weeks and we finally have an address," I said. "Will you take us?"

"I'd be glad to take you now. Your dad said it might be a while. I want to be near the phone this afternoon, but a person can't just sit around waiting all day," she said. "You all are good girls to return this to its rightful owners. I'm proud of you."

Zuzu smiled like she had just won a gold medal.

"Will your mom let you go to Helen's?" I asked Bella. I was afraid she would get grounded again.

"When I got home yesterday, Mom and I had a long talk," Bella said. "For the first time, I think she actually heard me and I think things are going to be different now." She smiled huge and bright. "My mom made honey ham for dinner, with cupcakes for dessert, just like she does when we have company. I asked her who was coming over and she said no one was. She said she wanted to make a special dinner just for the two of us. After that, we did the dishes together." Bella smiled so big, I hardly recognized her. "She asked if there was anything I wanted to do with her this weekend, and I said I wanted to take her to the art museum. She said she would be happy to go with me. My mom—at an art museum!"

Bella looked different. She looked confident. She stood up straight and looked me right in the eye when she spoke. She didn't seem like the girl who a few nights ago believed she was extra. She looked like Bella—Bella all the way.

Zuzu and I ate and got dressed. We all filed into Grandma's enormous Sahara-beige car. Bella, Zuzu and I sat in the backseat while Grandma Brooks hummed to herself in the front.

After a few minutes, we pulled into the driveway of a little brick house. It was tidy and looked well cared for. A pair of plastic deer rested near some bushes under the front window. We got out of the car and walked up to the porch. A little plastic hedgehog stood watch next to the front door.

I knocked. An old woman with short, curly silver hair and a twilight-blue housedress opened the door.

"Hi, um. Hi," I said.

"Hello. Can I help you?" she asked, opening the door a bit wider, but not all the way.

"Um. Is this . . . are you Helen White Phelps?" I asked.

"Yes," said the old lady.

Zuzu gasped and almost fell down the porch steps.

"We have something of yours we'd like to return," said Bella, holding out the journal wrapped in a plastic bag.

"What's this?" Helen said. She pulled out the journal, and then clapped her hand over her mouth. She swallowed hard like she was trying not to cry. She opened the door all the way and motioned for us to come in.

"Please, have a seat," she said. The house was warm with the same old-things feeling as Grandma's. Helen motioned for us to sit on various very old dusty-hills-green chairs and couches. An old man with thin strands of cottony hair sat in a recliner reading a newspaper. He didn't look up.

"This is my brother, Fred," she said, holding her hand out to the old man. He smiled and nodded.

"Freddy!" gasped Zuzu. He looked up at us and raised his thick cobweb eyebrows.

Helen sat down in a big recliner. She looked small. She opened the journal and scanned the entries. Her mouth moved as she read, but no sound came out. A large tear rolled down her cheek and caught in the valleys and folds of her wrinkles until it seemed to vanish. Another followed it.

"I never thought I'd see this again," she said, mostly to

herself. She looked up. "Who are you and where did you find this?"

We went around the little room and introduced ourselves. "Zuzu and I live in your old house," I said.

"We found the journal in Palace Beautiful," said Bella.

"My Palace Beautiful!" said Helen, her eyes wide and shining.

"Yes," said Bella, smiling almost as brightly as when Zuzu and I saw her on the lawn with Jason Prince.

"How is my Palace Beautiful?"

"We've fixed it up really nice," said Zuzu. "You should come over and see it."

"What's this Palace Beautiful?" asked Grandma.

"It's a little hiding place I made in the old house during a very hard time. It was my own little refuge," said Helen.

"We want to know what happened," said Zuzu.

"What happened?" said Helen.

"Yeah, what happened when the journal ended? What about Lizzy, Rachel and your dad?" asked Zuzu. "What happened with your mother and Anna?"

"And Martha," said Bella, "and Mrs. Phelps and Paul."

"Well, I can tell you what happened to Paul. He married me." She smiled so big I could tell her teeth were false.

"But I thought you didn't like him because he threw crab apples at you!" said Zuzu.

"Oh, he improved with age and so did I," said Helen.

"Is he here, too?" asked Zuzu.

"No, Paul passed away three years ago. Fred's wife, Lois,

passed away the next year, so he moved in here with me. That way we can keep an eye on each other."

"Will you tell us what happened with everyone?" Zuzu asked so eagerly, I thought she might fall off the couch. Helen looked at Freddy, and he smiled at her gently like he was urging her on.

"I'd love to hear a good story, too," he said. His voice was deep and dusty-old.

Helen opened the journal again and skimmed its pages. "I got sick," she said. "I don't know for how long. All I know is that the nurses from the Health Department came to the house and heard Freddy crying. They followed the sound and found us in Palace Beautiful. I was too sick to move, but Freddy stayed warm in my arms long after all the fires in the house went out and it was as cold as winter inside. They said that even though I was sick, I saved his life." Helen beamed proudly.

"That she did," said Freddy, nodding and smiling at Helen.

"It took a long time for me to heal—not just my body, but my heart. Some things, like a person losing their mother and sister, can never really heal. A person just learns to get on with things."

"Do you still have the red shawl?" asked Bella.

"No, they took it away when they took little Anna. I was never sure what they did with it. Wait just a minute."

Helen got up and walked down the hall. A few minutes later, she came back holding a pillow-feather-blue plastic bag. She handed it to me. "Open it," she said.

I did. I pulled out a very old doll with a porcelain head.

"Millie?" I gasped.

"Millie!" said Zuzu.

Helen nodded. I passed it to Zuzu and Bella. They fingered her china head reverently like it was a real baby.

"They left the doll when they took Anna away," Helen said. "Anyway, my father's and Lizzy's health improved quickly. Rachel and I were slower to recover, but we all healed eventually. Fred here never got sick."

"What happened to the Phelpses?" asked Bella, handing Millie back to Helen.

"Martha's family was hit hard. Mrs. Phelps got it first, I'm sure from caring for us. Her husband and Paul got easy cases of it, but Martha got it bad. She never fully recovered. When she came out of it, she had to learn to feed herself, walk and talk all over again. It was my after-school job to take care of her and be her companion for the rest of my school years. That is how Paul and I began to be real friends. Martha lived to be thirty years old. She never learned to walk without help or speak like normal again. I understood her, though. So did Paul. She lived with her parents until she died. For a few years after Paul and I got married, Martha and I got to be actual sisters like we'd always wanted."

"Where are Lizzy and Rachel now?" I asked, watching Helen hold Millie in her arms like she was holding little Anna again.

"Lizzy married a farmer from Montana. They moved up north to a ranch of their own and had four sons. Lizzy and her husband ran that farm for years and years. They sure had some happy times. They are retired now and enjoying their lives in the little town where they live.

"Rachel married a man from Emory County. They had three daughters and two sons. Her husband ran a law firm. When their children moved out, Rachel took up politics, of all things. She was the first woman mayor of their town. Her husband passed away last year, but she is still going strong. Freddy and I had her up for Thanksgiving last year.

"Paul and I married when I was eighteen. We bought this house and raised our daughters here. They are all good girls. Frances and Anna were easy and obedient. Lillian and Elizabeth were like Paul, and there was never a dull moment in this house. We have lots of grandchildren and great-grandchildren now. Paul worked for a construction company. I stayed home with my girls and enjoyed almost every minute."

"Almost?" said Zuzu, smiling.

"The crab apple doesn't fall far from the tree," Helen said, and she winked at Zuzu.

"What about your dad?" I asked.

"My father was so broken up after my mother's death that we moved a few months later. He couldn't stand to be in that house any longer with all those memories. We moved across town, but I spent my weekdays at school and lodging at the Phelpses' house. My father died six months after Rachel left home. He was always lonely for Mother until the end. He is buried in the city cemetery next to Mother and Anna."

"What about you, Freddy?" asked Zuzu. Freddy looked

up, a little startled, like he hadn't expected to be included in the conversation.

"Well," he said slowly. "After Father died, I moved up to Montana to live with Lizzy and her boys. I loved working the ranch with them. I loved running after the cattle and riding the horses. Her boys were just like my brothers. We had a grand time. When I was twenty-three, I married Lois. She was a pretty thing from Butte. We lived in Montana for four years and then moved back to Utah. I went to law school and set up a practice in town. Lois and I had two sons and a daughter. They all live here in the valley."

"Fred has lots of grandchildren and great-grandchildren now, too," said Helen.

"Helen," said Zuzu. "Would you like to see your Palace Beautiful again?"

"What?" said Helen, like Zuzu had just asked her if she would like to go back in time. "Well, I don't know," she said. "After the flu, I never went back up there again, except to hide my journal and shut it up for good. I made the place during a really hard time. It might be tough to see it again."

"But it might be wonderful," said Bella.

"Wisdom, indeed!" said Grandma Brooks.

"Fred, will you come with me?" asked Helen.

"Sure," said Freddy, rocking lazily in his chair.

"How about this afternoon for lunch?" asked Grandma.

Helen started like she hadn't expected anything so soon. She thought for a minute, and then said, "Might as well."

"All right. Lunch it is," said Grandma.

"Thank you so much for bringing me my old journal," said Helen, getting out of her chair to see us out. She moved slowly and with what looked like as much effort as Sherrie.

We all said good-bye and walked out to the driveway. The rain had stopped and everything smelled spicy, clean and new.

Moth-Wing Pink

BELLA WENT HOME WHEN WE GOT back to Grandma's. There was a message on Grandma's answering machine from Dad saying there was no change yet.

Grandma Brooks, assisted by Zuzu, redressed my hand in cotton gauze and wrapped it in a medical-peach stretchy bandage. It felt clean, tight and secure in a way that made me feel like everything was going to heal just fine.

Then the three of us went to our house to clean up the storm's mess. Zuzu held the dustpan as I moved the broom back and forth under my bedroom window. Grandma Brooks had covered the window with plastic to keep the weather outside until the window repairmen could fix it permanently.

Meeting Helen in real life felt so nice. So nice that I almost forgot about Sherrie being in the hospital. Helen and Freddy were both alive and healthy. They had lived through the influenza epidemic in this very house. They made it, and life just went on a new way. I looked at the bandage on my hand. It would be there for another week or two, then I could take it off and in a few more weeks it would be all the way healed. Suddenly I understood that if something did happen to Sherrie, it would hurt and burn and sting, but life would keep moving. It would just move in a different way. I lost my mom and that's what happened. Helen lost people she loved and she kept living. I realized that no matter how painful it would be, I could take it.

The wind blew outside, making the plastic window covering bow and contract. It didn't get inside, though. I peered through the blurry plastic and it looked like it was going to storm again. Kids were running home and the sycamore's leaves showed their white undersides. Inside, there was no wind and no storm. Sometimes, the world tries to get in. It bangs and pounds, and sometimes it even blows in and makes a mess. But somewhere, tucked behind the boxes and crates of living, there is always a Palace Beautiful waiting to be found.

I looked out again. Jason and Derrick were picking up their basketball to go inside. Derrick looked up and saw me peering out the window. He waved and I waved back.

Just then a big white van with the words DAVE'S WINDOW REPAIR pulled up in the driveway. Calamity mewed at my feet. I picked her up and rubbed her soft fur on my cheek and smiled.

That afternoon, Zuzu, Bella and I led Grandma Brooks, Helen and Freddy up the attic stairs.

When she saw the opening to the little room, Helen's eyes spilled over and tears again disappeared into the folds of her soft moth-wing-pink cheeks. We stood outside the entrance as Helen and Freddy bent down and crawled inside.

"Mother!" said Helen, touching the photo. "The candle!" she said. "Freddy, you were the only other person from our family to come up here. It was our safe place."

Freddy's eyes spilled over as he listened to Helen and looked at the photograph.

"Here," said Bella, picking up the red shawl. "We crocheted this and we all sewed it together. I think you should have it—to replace the one you lost." She wrapped the shawl around Helen's hunched shoulders.

"Thank you so much!" said Helen. "I will always treasure this."

"We all made it together," said Bella. "I got the pattern from a book called *Crochet in an Afternoon*. It was only supposed to take an afternoon, but it took us longer."

At that moment, I realized Bella wasn't from the Great Dog or Adam and Eve. She was from the red birds that sat on the branches of the mourning apple tree. She was one of the ones who fill the empty spaces. She had given me Calamity so I could have something soft when I missed my mom. She had crocheted with Grandma Brooks when most of her crochet friends had gone away. She had replaced the shawl Helen had lost. I looked at her and couldn't help smiling. I was glad she was my friend.

The phone rang. I was so caught up in everything that it took me a minute to realize it might be Dad and Sherrie.

Zuzu and I raced downstairs, with Zuzu darting ahead to get the phone before they hung up.

"Grandma! It's Dad!" shouted Zuzu.

Grandma Brooks picked up the phone and said, "Hello . . . yes . . . yes. . . . Today? How's Sherrie? Yes . . . yes."

She didn't look happy. She hung up. "Sherrie is having a bit of a bad time, but the doctors say they have it under control."

I looked outside. I wondered what was going on with Sherrie. Was she in pain? Was she scared? Were the doctors nice? How was my dad? How was the baby? I was old enough to know that no one, not even doctors, are ever really in control.

That night, in the guest room, I couldn't sleep. I picked up Calamity and tiptoed to the living room so I wouldn't wake anyone. I sat at the picture window and watched the stars slowly twist around the North Star until suddenly it was morning.

Honey Black

THE PHONE RANG. CALAMITY AND I were lying on the couch under the front window. It took me a minute to wake up all the way and remember how we got there. I heard Grandma Brooks answer the phone. Suddenly, I realized what the phone call could mean. I dashed into the kitchen. Zuzu sat at the breakfast table and I sat down next to her.

"Zuzu, this is it!" I said. She dropped her fork and it spun and clattered on the floor. We froze and tried to hear what Grandma was saying.

I was dying to hear what was going on, but at the same time, I didn't want to know.

"Do you think . . . do you think Sherrie is all right?" Zuzu asked.

"I don't know," I said, but I don't think she heard me.

"All right," said Grandma Brooks. "We'll be there. Give my love to Sherrie. . . . Okay, bye."

She hung up, and Zuzu and I sat in our kitchen chairs hardly breathing. It felt like everything slowed down and sped up at the same time. I wanted to know more than anything, and I didn't want to know more than anything, and everything in the universe jumbled and toppled over itself.

"Well," Grandma said. "Sherrie's had the baby!"

"YES!" shouted Zuzu. She tried to jump up, but banged her knees on the table and sat back down.

"Is she . . . how's Sherrie?" I asked.

"Sherrie is fine. Everything went well and she is happy and comfortable."

I felt my shoulders loosen. I hadn't realized they were tight. I wondered if I had been holding that anxiety the entire nine months. I felt so relieved, I started to cry. Grandma Brooks walked over and hugged me. She was soft. I held on to her until I could get hold of myself.

"Everything's fine, Sadie. Everything's fine," she whispered over and over. I believed her and cried out of happiness.

"Well," said Zuzu. "Is it a brother or sister?"

"Get dressed and let's go to the hospital to find out. Sherrie wants it to be a surprise."

"The big reveal!" exclaimed Zuzu, and she bounded from the table and up the stairs to get dressed.

I followed. In about thirty seconds we were both dressed and waiting at the front door for Grandma to get her keys. We hopped into the car and drove to the hospital.

The sun sat on top of one of the mountain peaks, making

long shadows stretch across the road. I watched the light and shadow flash past until we got to the hospital.

We walked down a long corridor until we got to their room. Grandma Brooks knocked and a nurse opened the door and let us in.

The room was dim and quiet. Dad sat in a hard plastic chair by the bed. He looked different. He smiled so big, he looked like he was just a boy. He looked so happy. I hoped he looked like that when Zuzu and I were born. I imagine he did.

Sherrie lay in the bed holding a little bundle. She looked different, too. She looked tired, but she also looked radiant— so happy she could hardly hold all of the happiness inside and it was seeping out of the corners of her mouth and the deep places in her eyes. She looked like she was actually glowing.

"Come on in, ladies," she said.

Zuzu, Grandma and I stepped in reverently, like we were walking into some kind of church or holy shrine.

"Have a seat, girls." She patted the end of her bed and we obeyed. Sherrie sat up and handed me the bundle. The baby squirmed and wriggled in the blanket. I moved a corner of the blanket and saw a shock of downy honey-black hair tied up in a tiny pink ribbon.

"It's a sister!" I said.

"Hooray!" shouted Zuzu. The baby started and began to cry. I handed her back to Sherrie. I had a new sister. I couldn't believe it, I had a new sister!

"I'd like y'all to meet Jacqueline Olivia Brooks. Our own little Jackie O."

"Can I hold her?" Zuzu asked, obviously trying to be quiet so as not to scare the baby.

"Of course," said Sherrie, handing her the baby.

"My sister." Zuzu touched her tiny face and rocked her gently. "You know, Jennifer Meyer doesn't have a baby sister. She is sure missing out!"

"Yes, she is," said Dad.

I peeked over Zuzu's shoulder at our new sister. She had big dark eyes and tiny rosebud lips. Her cheeks were fat and rosy. She squirmed and twisted her tiny little mouth like she was trying out her new face to see how it worked.

"I think she looks like Sadie," said Sherrie. "She has that pretty faraway look in her eyes. She's going to be a smart thing. I can see it. Besides, y'all are the same season."

Baby Jackie looked at me with her deep dark eyes and I knew her story. Sherry looked at me and smiled. She knew it, too.

Zuzu says no one can remember the day they were born, but I do. I looked at my new little sister squirming around in my arms and something inside me just knew she would remember, too.

We sat in the room for a long time, passing the baby around and smiling until our cheeks hurt. I asked Sherrie if I could take the baby into the hall for a minute. She said yes and she didn't even look nervous. That's what I love about Sherrie.

I took my sister in my arms and went out to where we could be alone. I held her up close so she could hear, and then did what I was sure Sherrie had already done. I whispered the story of the Great Dog into her tiny, brand-new ear.

HERRIE CARRIED BABY JACKIE ACROSS the threshold of our home a week later. Because she was born early, she'd had to stay at the hospital for a while. Sherrie and Dad were there every day, and Zuzu and I were there a lot.

It felt good to have baby Jackie home.

She grunted and fussed and made the cutest little sounds. She looked so sweet wrapped in the good-morning-pink hospital blanket—like she was a little present with a little bow on top. Earlier that day, Grandma Brooks helped Zuzu and me put Bonnie Mae–pink balloons and streamers in the nursery to welcome her home.

"Oh, Norman, look!" Sherrie said when she walked into the nursery. "Did you girls do this?"

"Yes," said Zuzu, beaming with pride.

"It looks beautiful! And the balloons are her season."

"Can I hold her?" I asked. I sat in the rocking chair and

Sherrie handed me the tiny bundle. I held her close and rocked her in the same chair where my mom held and rocked me when I was new. I held her close and rocked her in the same house where Helen had rocked little Freddy. I thought that someday, maybe baby Jackie would hold close and rock her own little bundle. For now, she was ours and she was beautiful. I inhaled. She smelled like new. She smelled wonderful.

Later that day, I had Sherrie hold Jackie in that chair and I painted their portrait. I filled the paper with home-sweet-home yellows and blues. I used brand-new pink and rosy-cheek red. It was my favorite portrait I'd ever painted. Dad said he would have it framed and hang it in the living room.

Helen came by to see the baby a few days later. She brought presents. For the baby she brought a whisper-yellow and far-far-away-blue crocheted bear with button eyes and a pink ribbon around its neck. For Zuzu, Bella and me she brought journals.

"Thank you!" Zuzu, Bella and I said in unison.

Helen smiled and said, "You never know when what you write can change things for someone else. Some things should never be forgotten."

After Helen left, Bella, Zuzu and I took our new journals up to Palace Beautiful. We lit the candle and wrote our first entries. I wrote:

August 5, 1985
 My name is Sadie Evelyn Brooks. I'm thirteen years old and practically a woman. The first thing a person

remembers is their story—the story of how they came into being. Mine goes like this:

In the beginning, there was nothing, no light, no dark, no air—nothing. Then, suddenly, a Great Dog as big as the universe came into being and then there was something.

ACKNOWLEDGMENTS

With special thanks to my wonderful agent, Erin Murphy, and my exceptional editor, Susan Kochan, without whom this book would have never left my home. Thanks to the ladies of my Phoenix book group for teaching me how to get to the meat of a story. Thanks to my husband and kids for encouraging me and allowing me the time and space to pursue my dreams. Thanks to all my writer friends who helped me keep my chin up when things were hard and celebrated with me when things were good.

Discussion Questions

If you had a Palace Beautiful in your house, where would you want it to be? What would you do in it? Who would you invite to come with you?

Do you think the Williams family will see Helen and Freddy again? What do you think they could do together?

If your family were quarantined, what would you do to pass the time? What if there was no electricity?

What is the history of the place where you live? What do you know about who lived there? If you don't know what happened where you live, what could you do to find out?

What helps Sadie have a good relationship with her stepmother? How is it different from Bella's relationship with her mother?

How do the characters in the book deal with the hard things that happen to their family or friends?